HIS CHRISTMAS SWEATER

C.M. VALENCOURT

Copyright © 2018 C.M. Valencourt

All rights reserved. No part of this book may be reproduced in any form or by any electronic or mechanical means, including information storage and retrieval systems, without permission in writing from the publisher, except by reviewers, who may quote brief passages in a review.

Cover Design by Cate Ashwood, cateashwooddesigns.com.

Printed in the United States of America.

Visit cmvalencourt.com.

CONTENTS

Chapter 1	1
Chapter 2	5
Chapter 3	13
Chapter 4	21
Chapter 5	31
Chapter 6	39
Chapter 7	51
Chapter 8	57
Chapter 9	65
Chapter 10	77
Chapter 11	83
Epilogue	91
Afterword	99

FROM THE ASHES

Chapter 1	103
Chapter 2	111
About the Author	117
Also by C.M. Valencourt	119

CHAPTER 1

*O*wen Campbell's heart rate jumped to what he assumed were medically dangerous levels as his late-model SUV fishtailed for the second time this trip. The snow was only getting worse and the roads had been hazardous for at least the past five miles.

Shit! Owen thought. *I knew I should have left before it got too dark to see my own damn headlights.*

The drive to Owen's parents' house in Eagle, Colorado usually took just over two hours from his apartment in Denver. But with the worsening conditions slowing I-70 down to a crawl, he was already past the two-hour mark but less than half of the way there.

It'll be New Year's before I get there at this rate, Owen thought, trying to keep both his temper and pulse under control. It was just after 9 p.m. on Friday, December 22nd. Owen wanted to spend as much time with his family as possible, and this shitty weather was seriously cutting into the festivities. The drive to his parents' house was stressful enough without risking life and limb trying to drive through the mountains in a blizzard.

He was just outside Silverthorne, still about sixty miles out, when the emergency alert interrupted a particularly ironic rendition of "Winter Wonderland."

"This is an emergency alert from the National Weather Service. Central Colorado is currently experiencing extreme winter storm conditions. Motorists travelling on westbound I-70 are instructed to pull off and seek shelter. The Colorado Department of Transportation warns conditions are too severe for safe travel."

"Fuck me running!" Owen shouted at nothing and everything at once. There was no way to get to his parents' tonight if they're closing the freeway. And he had to admit he couldn't really remember trying to drive in conditions quite this hostile. He hated to stop when he was so close, but he'd already passed three or four cars that had lost control and slid into the treacherous ditch on the side of the road. Even his four-wheel drive was losing traction in this mess.

He passed two more exits before he saw a sign advertising a hotel he could actually afford. The mountains west of Denver are prime skiing country, and he wasn't going to drop $500 on a five-star chalet just to wait out the storm.

Owen couldn't call the sorry collection of weather-beaten buildings that greeted him a *town*, exactly, but the dozen or so cabins and double-wides he could make out from the white and multicolored twinkle lights adorning every eave looked a hell of a lot cozier than the layer of snow his defrost couldn't quite keep off the windshield. He knew that feeling homesick less than eighty miles away from where you live was ridiculous, but his sudden longing for Denver's salted roads and abundant streetlights sat like a solid lump in his gut.

Luckily, Owen quickly spotted the only hotel serving the little hamlet: a local single-story inn called Elk Terrace Lodge. He couldn't help but notice the conspicuous lack of any decorations as he pulled in. He supposed hotels didn't *need* to be decked out in lights and wreaths on every square inch, but these kinds of mom-and-pop inns usually went all out for the season. Still, it was either this or freezing in his car. There was no way he was getting back on the road tonight.

He grabbed his overnight bag out of the backseat and headed toward the already snow-buried front steps of the lodge.

CHAPTER 2

"If you'll all just wait one minute, I have to take this call from the owner," Jacob Parker shouted just loud enough to be heard over the din. He had to restrain himself from running toward the office phone and the door he could close on the mob of disgruntled holiday travelers stranded in the blizzard.

Why did these people think driving through the mountains in a snowstorm was a good idea anyway? he thought. *Can't they just check the forecast and stay home?*

Jacob took a moment to breathe, grateful for a brief escape from the sudden chaos of the hotel lobby.

The office phone, now on its fourth ring, swelled to fill the silence Jacob hoped to revel in for half a second longer. If he waited much longer, Ethel, Elk Terrace's septuagenarian proprietor, would be on his ass too, and despite occasionally overhearing guys evaluate it as "nice" and "perfectly filling out his jeans" the poor thing was running out of real estate.

"Elk Terrace Lodge, this is Jacob. How may I help you?" he answered politely. He knew it wasn't a prospective guest, but Ethel maintained what she called "a passion for telephone etiquette." If the caller couldn't see the brown on your nose from across the phone lines, you weren't trying hard enough.

"Oh, *there* you are, Jake." She managed to convey annoyance at being kept waiting in the exact tone his grandmother used to offer him candy from her purse.

Lost for a moment wondering at the talent some possess to coat displeasure in a sugary shell, Jake realized that he had missed something important and now couldn't supply the reaction she was clearly waiting for.

"I'm sorry, Ethel, but what's happening now?

"The storm, Jake! All this snow. Officer Larson from highway patrol just called to inform me that they're closing I-70 due to unsafe conditions."

Oh perfect, he thought. *Now even the guests who were trying to leave to beat the weather will be demanding my head.*

"Ethel, I've got a hoard of holiday travelers out here chomping at the bit to get on the road before the snow ruins their Christmas." Jake fought to keep his mounting anxiety out of his voice.

"You tell 'em there is no more before. The only way in or out has been buried under ten tons of powdery bullshit! Colin Peters on Channel Four says there's no sign of it letting up anytime soon. Said something about a *polar blast*. Go on and offer the guests the extended stay discount, and if they get too riled up, tell 'em that I'm sure ol' Bob McNamara down at the Citgo would be glad to let 'em stay overnight in the outhouse."

He chuckled at the rare crack in Ethel's famous "Christian disposition."

"Aye aye, Captain. But, uh, Ethel, I sure could use some help here."

"No can do, Jake. The mountain road has gone all tundra

on me, and even if I wanted to pull Sylvie back from her family Christmas, she'd have to snowshoe all the way here from Grand Junction."

Ethel was from hardy mountain stock, as she loved reminding people. She usually loved the cold and snow, not like those cold-blooded snowbird types that need to bask in the sun all year round or they'll shrivel up. If *she* thought the snow was too bad to get here, it must have been well and truly fucked out there.

"Looks like it's just you and Amanda holding down the fort until this lets up."

Mandy was the Lodge's seasonal housekeeper, a disaffected UC Boulder student who had spent every summer and winter break since high school at Elk Terrace playing on her phone in the supply closet and trying to promote her own highly questionable definition of "clean" one guest bathroom at a time. Jacob enjoyed her spunk and even appreciated her help during the approximately two minutes per day he could convince her to actually do work, but most of all, he liked having an ally in the constant war between him and the guests.

"Alright, I guess we'll make do." Jake sighed, the full-body tension that had been building for several minutes now hardening into a hard lump of bitterness in his stomach. But he couldn't say no to Ethel. Ever since coming to work at Elk Terrace, she had basically adopted him. She tried to make sure he was eating enough to fit her definition of well fed, she took an interest in what he was feeling on any given day, and she even tried to set him up with guys she considered to be "eligible bachelors." Not that a seventy-six year old straight woman's definition of a potential romantic partner exactly matched up with his twenty-seven-year-old gay man's, but the thought still brought a comfortable, warm feeling to his chest.

"You remember your manners when dealing with our guests, Jacob Parker, you hear?"

"Sure thing, Ethel. Anything else I can do to assist you this fine midwinter's night?" Jake said in his most gracious, servile, and vaguely British voice.

"You keep that up and I'll get Santa himself to drive me to the Lodge to give you a piece of my mind," Ethel tried to snap, but she chuckled in spite of herself.

"Oh, and Jake? Merry Christmas," she ended with a note of finality.

"Bah humbug!" Jake shouted into the phone, hoping she heard it as she reached to hang up the receiver on her ancient rotary dial.

Well, I suppose it's now or never, he thought, bracing himself for the onslaught of now-stranded holiday travelers. One more deep breath, and then he had to step through the door and ruin Christmas.

~

The lobby was crowded when Jacob stepped out of the office. He recognized most of the faces as guests that were chomping at the bit to check out and hit the road—they were in for a nasty shock—but he also spotted two or three new people who must have come in looking to wait out the storm. Maybe they would go easy on him.

"If I can have everyone's attention please," Jacob shouted above the grumbling crowd, turning quickly hostile. "I just received news from the highway patrol. I–70 has been closed due to all the snow."

A chorus of complaints rang out and Jacob considered

running back to the office and barricading the door with the human-sized Santa statue Ethel insisted they keep around "to keep us in the holiday spirit." He fought to suppress a slightly hysterical laugh. If she could see this mob, maybe she's change her tune on the whole good will toward men business.

"We have also been advised that the mountain road is already blocked off by the accumulation."

"So what the fuck are we supposed to do?" a middle-aged man demanded with an expression so furious it made Jacob glad that he didn't live in a stand-your-ground state.

"Elk Terrace is happy to offer all of our guests our extended stay discount while we wait out the-"

"Hey asshole, we don't want to stay another second in this dump. I gotta get home and give my kids a Christmas," the man shouted. The conflict seemed to settle the crowd a bit, no one wanting to take sides with either Jacob or the unreasonably hostile man.

"Sir, if you would like to check out, that is of course your right, but the only way in or out of town is blocked off by the worst snow we've seen in thirty years. If you want to take your chances out in the blizzard, be my guest. Everyone else, I can help check you in up front." Jacob smiled to himself at the slightly horrified look that replaced the fury on the man's face. If he had to deal with the bullshit weather, he wasn't about to let himself get bullied by some fucking tourist. *Besides,* he thought. *With that attitude your kids probably have a much better chance of feeling some Christmas joy without you.* Jacob understood the appeal of the whole big family Christmas in theory, but the reality always seemed more stressful and less fulfilling than the movies led you to believe.

As soon as he managed to strike the fear of God and hypothermia in the hearts of the masses, the line started to move fairly smoothly. Ten minutes of rapid-fire check-ins later and the lobby was starting to empty.

"Next!" Jacob called without even looking up from the computer. "How may I help you?"

"One room and a heaping helping of your best figgy pudding," returned the first voice he'd heard all night without a bite of anger, accusation, or panic in it.

He looked up to see who the voice belonged to and *holy shit*. His mind instantly filled with two very discordant thoughts trying to scream over each other. *Oh great, a city slicker who's probably never set foot in a small town, showing up here dressed like he just lost a fight with an Armani catalog and wearing a goddamn* Santa hat *no less,* the bitter, mountain man part of his brain supplied. But another, insubordinate part of his brain couldn't help but notice how his blue-green eyes seemed to twinkle, and how his full face and soft features conveyed kindness and warmth.

Jacob snapped to a few moments later when a puzzled expression from the man across from him signaled that he'd been gawking for a beat too long.

"Uh... we don't offer dinner service here," Jacob said while he internally smacked himself for sounding so dumbstruck.

"Wha–? Oh!" The man chuckled. "Just the room then."

"Right," Jacob said, scrambling to shake off whatever haze was turning him into a babbling idiot. Maybe there was a carbon monoxide leak, and he was mere seconds from dropping dead.

"Can I get your name?"

"Owen Campbell. And yours?"

Jacob squinted at Owen's grin.

"Jacob Parker. Single or double?" he asked, thankful for

the barrier of the front desk and his calculated professionalism.

"It's just me. I would *not* like to take my chances with the blizzard." Jacob smiled at him. "Oh, and is there a Starbucks near here? I am desperate for a peppermint hot chocolate."

Jacob had to physically restrain himself from rolling his eyes. As far as he knew, the gas station in town didn't even carry the Starbucks drinks in the little glass bottles. He gave the city boy a generous twelve hours of being trapped on the mountain before he lost it.

"I think the nearest Starbucks is back in Denver," Jacob said hoping that he successfully kept the contempt out of his voice. His eyes kept darting up to that stupid Santa hat. He knew how to deal with grouchy travelers, snobby skiers, and even the occasional sleazy trucker, but Owen's particular brand of cosmopolitan entitlement and gratingly polite holiday cheer was something Jacob didn't have antibodies for. He was about to give Owen directions to the bourgie ski chalet a few miles down the road when he remembered Ethel and how hard she fought to keep their little shack up and running.

"However, we can provide you with some instant hot cocoa mix to make in your coffee pot."

"That sounds perfect." Owen's smile was warm and appreciative, and Jacob could swear he heard Ethel's voice just over his shoulder saying, "See? Folks respond well when you're kind to them."

"Just ask Mandy, our housekeeper, and she'll get you set up with everything you need." Jacob passed Owen the key and stared intently down at the computer to hide the rising blush from projecting his embarrassment at the whole stupid interaction.

"And thank you for choosing Elk Terrace Lodge."

"Thank you for saving me from the apocalypse." Owen turned to go find his room. "And happy holidays!" he shouted to Jacob, but also to the world at large.

Jacob prayed the snow would let up soon so he could get these people, especially Owen, out of his hotel and out of his life.

CHAPTER 3

"*All major roadways, including I–70 remain closed today as record amounts of snow continue to fall across central Colorado. Holiday traffic is at a standstill with no end in sight. Flights have been canceled at both the Denver International Airport and the Colorado Springs Municipal Airport as visibility remains at near zero. With Christmas only two days away, thousands of stranded holiday travelers find themselves praying for a Christmas miracle. This is Beverley Albright, Channel 8 News.*"

Owen turned off the TV. He stared out the window at the screen of featureless white snow that had blanketed the tiny mountain town overnight. It was falling so hard, he could barely make out the lights from the gas station he knew was just across the street. Normally he loved the snow, but if this kept up, he'd be stuck here until spring.

Determined to make the best of things, Owen put on one of his most festive sweaters, featuring two pine trees performing a Fred Astaire-style dance with candy canes and tree-topper stars instead of top hats, and for good measure, his Santa hat. He needed breakfast, and he had already gone through both mini packets of coffee that came with the room. *Maybe I can get that cute night manager to tell me where I can get something decent to eat,* he thought. One last look in the mirror to check that his hair was suitably tousled, and he headed down the hall to find breakfast.

He was surprised by the number of people he found milling around the small buffet nook off the lobby. He didn't quite realize how many people were in the same bad position as himself. The meager selection of bagels and fresh fruit that comprised the Elk Terrace continental breakfast was disappointing, but the coffee was hot and strong, and it managed to soothe some of Owen's mounting anxiety. He glanced around at the other blizzard refugees and was taken aback by how on edge everyone seemed.

Feeling claustrophobic, Owen refilled his coffee and turned to explore the hotel. He walked to the large picture window by the fireplace. It really was coming down out there, probably worse than last night. The wind was blowing the new snow into a flurry, so he couldn't even see to the end of the parking lot. *This is really bad,* he thought, dread beginning to creep into his stomach. He was starting to lose hope that he'd be able to leave today. He had to find something to distract himself; getting in his own head and freaking himself out wasn't going to make the storm pass any faster. Turning away to survey the lobby, he noticed the manager. Jacob, he remembered. There were worse ways to kill time than chatting up a broody, lumberjack type.

Owen was about to walk up and talk to Jacob when he heard the 8-bit rendition of "Sleigh Ride," the most annoying song he could find that was still technically festive, which he reserved for his parents' ringtone.

"Hi, Mom"

"Owen, where are you? We've been worried sick! When you tell people that you're going to be here at a certain time, they expect you at that time. Your father and I have been killing ourselves trying to get everything ready for–"

"Whoa, Mom, slow down." He cut her off before her tirade could get too much momentum.

"I'm stranded at a hotel about eighty miles outside of Denver."

"Why on earth are you at a hotel? Your sister and her kids have been here all morning and you promised them that they would get to spend the weekend with their uncle who they never get a chance–"

"Uh, hello? Have you not seen the news? Blizzard of the century? Highway closed for the duration? Any of that ringing a bell? I'm snowed in here."

"Watch your tone with me, young man. A little winter weather is no excuse to talk to me like I'm an idiot. What do you mean snowed in? How bad can it be?"

His parents lived in a postage stamp-sized town in Eagle County, on the west side of the larger mountains. The weather tended to be pretty different over there.

"There's no way to get through the mountains until they reopen the roads. Until the snow lets up I'm on standby. I'm sorry."

"Oh, honey, I'm sorry! We already hung the stockings, and the kids are out doing the snowball fight right now."

Owen felt a twinge of disappointment at the thought of missing out on some of his favorite Campbell family traditions. Even though Christmas at his parents' house tended to be stressful, with the children running through the small, modest house like bulls in a pottery shop and his mother's constant badgering about finding work closer to home, maybe something in Grand Junction, he looked forward to it every year like he was still eight years old and anxiously waiting to see what kind of presents Santa had in mind this year.

"Will you make it in time for the Christmas cookie bake off?"

"I don't know, Mom. I hope so."

"Well, if you'd left yesterday morning, like I told you to, you would have been here long before the blizzard started."

He rolled his eyes. *And if you didn't insist on living in West Buttfuck Nowhere, I wouldn't have to drive through a blizzard to get there.* He took a cleansing breath.

"I left as soon as I could. Maybe next year Santa will send me the power to psychically predict the weather."

"Very funny, smartass. Keep that up and we won't save any of the gingerbread for you."

Owen knew she was only half kidding, but he decided not to press his luck. His mother's gingerbread was world class, and probably the best thing he ate all year.

"Ok, Mom, I'll call you when the roads open up. But just in case, tell everyone I said Merry Christmas, and I love them."

They said their goodbyes and Owen could feel the reality of his situation closing in on him. He'd never missed a family Christmas before. He wouldn't be able to hear his father's grumbly baritone as the family gathered around the tree to sing carols, or see the look on his nephews' faces as they tore into their presents. Owen caught himself reaching up to wipe away a tear forming in the corner of his eye.

"Hey, man, are you okay?"

Owen started, turning to see who caught him fucking *crying*.

"Oh," Owen said, looking into Jacob's warm, chocolate

eyes. "Uh, yeah." He tried to mask wiping away another tear behind a stretch and yawn, but Jacob cocked his head slightly to the left, clearly seeing right through Owen's ruse.

"I guess everyone's a little on edge about the road closures," Owen said, downplaying his own disappointment.

"Yeah, travel delays are never fun," Jacob said far too casually than was appropriate for the situation, Owen thought.

"Yeah," Owen began in a tone that reminded him of explaining the punchline of a bad joke. "And the whole maybe missing Christmas thing."

"Oh. That." Jacob seemed almost totally uninterested in the idea of spoiling the most wonderful time of year. "Is that what your call was about?"

Owen detected a slight uptick in the pitch of his voice that he chose to interpret as concern.

"It was my mother, asking me when I was going to be there and informing me that they've already started some of the Campbell family traditions without me."

"That sucks, man. I'm sorry."

Owen smiled with only a tinge of bitterness.

"And now it's not looking like the storm is gonna let up at all today, so I'll probably miss Christmas Eve, and maybe the big day, and I haven't seen my sister Zoe or her kids since last year, because they were at the kids' dad's for Thanksgiving, and now I'm worried that I won't be able to get their presents to them on time, and they don't get a chance to receive too many nice things, and—"

Owen sniffled a bit. He had no intention of breaking down in front of the totally hot, if annoyingly indifferent desk guy, but his resolve was shaking. He didn't realize how many separate emotions he'd attached to this particular Christmas. The one he was probably going to miss. He tried to get his breathing under control before he started violently sobbing in a hotel lobby.

"Hey, hey, hey, it's okay." Jacob slung his arm around Owen, a note of concern in his voice. "Who knows if this storm is even gonna last through today. They could have the roads ready to go before dark."

Owen sniffed.

"Yeah, that's true," he said, trying to retake control of his shaky voice.

"And besides," Jacob continued, removing his arm from Owen's shoulder. The loss of the warmth and pressure nearly sent a fresh wave of sorrow through Owen. "Christmas is only one day, right? You can give your family presents anytime."

Owen wanted to explain that it wasn't that simple. That two big family dinners at the end of the year was usually the only time everyone could get together because he lived and worked on the east side of the state, and his sister stayed in northern California with the kids so the tenuous joint custody agreement with her ex didn't escalate into a full-on legal battle. But Jacob was just some guy who ran a hotel in the woods. He didn't need to hear all twenty-five years of Owen's family drama. His gruff, blasé attitude toward the holiday season didn't inspire much confidence, either.

"Hey, can I ask something?" Owen asked, shifting the subject away from his emotional baggage.

"Why aren't there any Christmas decorations in this place?" he continued when Jacob didn't say no. "Usually these little mountainside inns are decked out like the 34th street Macy's."

"Oh," Jacob wrinkled his nose at the mere implication of Manhattan. "Right. Well, Ethel, the owner, usually takes care of all that, but she hasn't been around much this winter. It's been difficult for her to make it all the way down here these days. No one else stepped up to do it."

Owen still couldn't believe how little this guy seemed to care, or even to notice the holiday season happening around him.

"Don't you think it's a little dreary in here? For the season, I mean."

"I'm making a killing on all this overtime and holiday pay. By the time the roads are clear, I could have enough to buy this place. I'd work in a cave all year for that kind of return. Anyway, holiday decorations are always too loud and bright and–" He trailed off with a sort of sweeping gesture.

Owen decided right then that even though he was curious about Jacob's weird aversion to festivity, his grinch act was altogether too depressing for them to really be friends.

"I guess I'll go get settled into my room," Owen said, officially over this whole weird interaction. "If I'm gonna be stuck here for a while, that is. Uh, thanks, for talking me through that whole–" He waved in an all-encompassing gesture similar to Jacob's.

Jacob mumbled some sort of reply, but Owen had already turned, walking back to his room and whistling the "Carol of the Bells" loud enough, he hoped, to annoy the front desk grinch.

He smiled to himself, imagining the look of intense cynical brooding that must be creeping over that stupid, perfectly sharp jawline.

CHAPTER 4

*J*acob was relieved to feel the warmth on his face when he closed the back door against the piercing wind. It was worse out there than it looked from the frosted windows.

"Where the *hell* have you been?" Mandy, the housekeeper on duty demanded of him.

Figures. The first time he'd seen or heard from her all day, and she's on the verge of a breakdown.

"I took the snowmobile to the market. I figured the guests would want something besides bagels and yogurt for dinner." He didn't mean to sound as defensive as he did.

"You've been gone for three hours! I've had to pacify the crowd, and I'm pretty sure Seventeen has been having the same panic attack since last night. Oh, and I haven't gotten a chance to change my clothes or shower or anything, because I'm trapped in a blizzard like Laura fucking Ingalls."

Jacob had already had his fill of heightened emotions dealing with the guests this morning. Still, Mandy was his only ally in the FEMA camp his sleepy mountain inn had suddenly become, and he was desperate for a friendly face amid the chaos.

"You should learn their names," he blurted out, not quite sure what he was going to say until it happened.

"I should what?" Mandy seemed as surprised as he was, and he hoped that she wouldn't turn on him too.

"The guests. We're probably gonna be here a while, and it'll be easier on us if we don't just refer to them by room number."

Mandy actually laughed.

"Wow, Jake. You become a bonafide Ethel in an emergency. Who woulda guessed?" She smiled at him, teasing, and he knew that she was on his side.

"You'd do well to take a page from her book too," he scolded as gently as he could, and affecting his best old lady voice and mimicking Ethel's slight hunch, he said, "Now be a dear and help my old bones bring these groceries into the kitchen."

They both laughed as they loaded their arms with the provisions and headed down the hall.

The kitchen in Elk Terrace wasn't designed with room service in mind. The single refrigerator and standard home range were usually just enough to get out a continental breakfast in the busy season, and to bake some cookies or muffins whenever Ethel felt "in a domestic way." Still, they managed to find places for the various cans, boxes, and the few fresh things Jake managed to get.

Seeing it all together, he felt a nagging insecurity in his shopping abilities. He was more of a frozen dinners and cold cut sandwiches kind of guy, himself. He didn't have much exposure to elaborate meal prep, except what he could infer from the few times a month that Ethel insisted the whole hotel gang come to her house for a "staff meeting," which mostly meant being fed more than they could possibly eat and enjoying one too many glasses of the expensive brandy she always seemed to have in endless supply, playing pinochle or gin rummy until Ethel fell asleep in her chair.

"So, you also brought someone to turn all this junk into dinner, right?" Mandy had been mercifully quiet about his lack of meal planning ability so far, and even though she was being her normal sarcastic self, the validity of her concern assured him it wasn't entirely directed at him.

"Yeah, I left Rachael Ray waiting out in a snowbank," he deadpanned. "I guess we'll have to figure something out."

"You'd better get to Googling," Mandy said from behind him. "Oh, that's right, the snow wiped out the internet."

"Wait, what?" Jake couldn't conceal the panic in his voice. He turned to see Mandy heading out the kitchen door. That was the only gripe Jacob had with rural mountain towns: the aerial cables used to run internet through the mountains were regularly at the mercy of high altitude weather.

"Merry Christmas!" she said in a mock-cheerful voice as she waved dismissively behind her.

Jacob felt his shoulders tense into knots.

~

"No, I'm sorry, Mrs., uh… King," Jacob struggled to match the guests' names with their various complaints. "The cable company won't be able to fix the internet until the snow lets up. Apparently all the weight from the snow brought a branch down on the line."

"Well, how the hell am I supposed to talk to my grandchildren who are upset that Grandma isn't there to spend Christmas with them?"

"I am terribly sorry, Mrs. King," Jacob tried not to growl

at the accusatory tone she was using, even though this couldn't be less his fault. "I asked them to please put us on the top of the list for service."

"I'm getting out of here as soon as I can!" Mrs. King shouted, before slamming the old-fashioned rotary phone that Ethel insisted gave each room "a familiar, classic feel."

"Good luck," he said as the receiver hit the cradle.

"Guests giving you hell today?"

Jacob looked up to see Owen in a much better mood, almost determined to be chipper and festive despite his near breakdown earlier that day.

"Uh, yeah. Some people seem to think that small-town hotel managers should be able to control the weather." Owen smiled, and Jacob felt a stab of panic at the warmth rising in his chest. Just because it had been a while since he'd been with anyone didn't mean that he had to turn to mush the second a mildly attractive dude grinned at him.

"Does your sweater…light up?" Jacob asked derisively, trying to throw some ice water onto the desire and embarrassment heating up his cheeks.

"Oh, yeah it does." Owen gave a soft laugh. "It even does," he fumbled with the hem around the back of the sweater. "This!" The sweater began to play a music box rendition of "Jingle Bell Rock".

"That's really something," Jacob scoffed. He immediately wished he hadn't said it, as he saw Owen's face darken with disappointment and suspicion.

"You're really not a Christmasy kinda guy, huh?" Owen was looking at Jacob in a way that made him feel like he was a puzzle that Owen was determined to crack.

"Right now, Christmas is what has me walking on eggshells trying to serve two dozen guests that treat me like I just killed their puppy right in front of their kids. So I'm waiting for December 26th like twinks wait for new Gaga albums."

Owen laughed with gusto at that, and Jacob scolded himself for making such a revealing comment so flippantly. He never consciously meant to float the whole *yeah I'm gay, and maybe I think you're hot* thing, right?

"I think the twinks have moved on to Carly Rae Jepsen or Lana Del Rey these days," Owen said with a grin that Jacob interpreted as *I'm gay too; glad we cleared that up*.

Just as their banter was creeping up on the danger zone of flirting, they were interrupted by one of the guests milling around the lobby bursting into tears. Jacob gave a quiet sigh equal parts relieved and frustrated. Luckily some of the other guests had already gathered around to comfort the woman sobbing about how her children would never forgive her for ruining the holiday. Jacob was glad he wasn't immediately responsible for calming the guest down, but the moment he'd shared with Owen, which, under torture, he might admit to enjoying, was definitely over.

Owen was staring at the developing scene, and Jacob swore he could hear the wheels turning in his mind.

"We've gotta do something to cheer these people up," Owen said, snapping out of his reverie.

"Like what?"

"We have to decorate," Owen said. "You *must* have some kind of decorations around here."

"Uh, I think there are some boxes in the basement," Jacob said, taken aback by the force of Owen's resolve.

"You have a basement?" Owen sounded incredulous.

"For storage." Jacob shrugged.

"Well, let's get going!"

Jacob quickly called Mandy, and threatened her with drumming up some entertainment for the guests if she didn't take the desk.

~

*J*acob watched in admiration as Owen dug through box after box of decorations they brought up from the little basement cellar. It was like he alone could make sense out of the tangle of lights, the endless knots of garland and tinsel. It was several minutes before Jacob even realized that he was sorting the contents into different piles, carefully grouped by type and color. Some of the other guests had gathered to watch Owen work.

It wasn't long before a big fake tree was erected in the lobby and the woman who had been crying, along with a few of the other more downtrodden guests, were given a large box of baubles and ornaments, as well as several strings of lights, and told to make it Santa proud.

Then he told Mandy to get all of the scissors and printer paper in the office and spread them out on the big coffee table in front of the fireplace. He invited the three unfortunate children who wound up stuck in the hotel two days before Christmas with their respective parents to make as many paper snowflakes as they could. Jacob was amused to see a few of the adults without children pick up pairs of scissors too.

Starting to get caught up in the decorating fever, Jacob popped into the office and came out with the Santa statue, setting it by the front desk as though to welcome any new visitors to the hotel.

Everyone gave a cheer when Jacob, at Owen's insistence,

hoisted the star up to the highest branch while Mandy, shaken from her teenage apathy by the new energy coursing through Elk Terrace, switched the normal anodyne muzak that Ethel loved to play in the lobby to an upbeat Christmas playlist by top 40 artists.

Jacob was about to walk over and congratulate Owen on all of his hard work when Owen sprang up with a box in his arm, and tore down the hallway like a whirlwind placing adhesive hooks with wreaths on all of the doors. Jacob took the initiative to place a long garland of fir branches and holly sprigs along the front desk. Before he could talk himself out of it, he stood up on the desk and pinned a tiny bundle of fake mistletoe tied with red and gold ribbon to the ceiling above his chair.

He climbed down just in time to see Owen returning from wreath duty. Owen looked too distracted to notice the work Jacob had just done, and he blushed when he realized that he put up the mistletoe just to see Owen's reaction.

"Hey, Jake, are there any candles we could set out?"

Jacob's breath hitched at the casual tone in Owen's voice. He didn't realize they were on a nickname basis, but it made him grin in spite of himself.

"Christmas isn't the same without some dancing candlelight to make everything feel warm and alive."

A stubborn, bitter part of himself gagged at the cheese factor of "dancing candlelight," but a softer, larger part, one that had thawed a bit from the warmth Owen was bringing to the lodge, decided to play along.

"There are some emergency candles in the supply room," he said. "They're not very decorative, but we might as well use 'em. If there's an emergency bigger than the one we're already in, a few candles won't make much difference."

They put candles in cheap plastic holders on every flat surface in the lobby. The desk ended up with so many, Jacob considered breaking out the spare fire extinguisher. They placed a candle in every window, and carefully moved up the paper snowflakes the kids had taped there. Soon, the whole lobby was twinkling and glowing. When the final ornaments were placed on the tree, Owen surveyed the room, taking in the results. He smiled, looking satisfied.

"Alright, who's hungry?" Jacob asked. Some of the guests actually cheered. He felt a stab of guilt when he told them the lodge didn't have anything more exciting to offer than cold cuts and chips. He could feel complaints forming on their lips and braced himself. Then Owen spoke up.

"I think that sounds great!" he said with more enthusiasm than anyone had ever felt about Jacob's cooking. He hoped they wouldn't mind that his culinary abilities didn't extend much past making frozen pizza or reheating leftovers of whatever casserole Ethel sent him home with that week. If the hero of the moment could accept Jacob's meager offering, the rest of them could too.

"Would you like some help getting things ready?" one of the tree-decorating women offered.

"That would be great. Thank you."

Jacob flashed Owen a smile that he hoped conveyed how grateful he was for the way he managed to turn the whole day around, and Owen smiled back softer and brighter than all the candles.

~

nce they had all eaten, Owen leaned over to whisper in Jacob's ear.

"I need your help in the kitchen," he breathed. "I have one more surprise for everyone."

Jacob shuddered at the closeness. Owen smelled amazing. Like warm winter spices and a leftover hint of pine from the wreaths. At that moment, he realized, nothing sounded better than getting a minute alone with this goofy, hyper-festive, very attractive man.

CHAPTER 5

*I*n the kitchen, Owen set about making his grandmother's hot chocolate recipe from scratch. He'd taken a minute to search the kitchen when he was hanging up wreaths, so he knew what he had to work with. He mixed the cocoa powder and sugar together, along with a few of Grandma's special ingredients, while Jacob warmed up a whole gallon of milk on the stove.

"How do you know how to do this?" Jacob asked. Owen noticed Jacob staring at him like he was working a miracle.

"Campbell family tradition." He flashed a bemused smile. "My grandma refused to pay for premade mix. She said she wasn't about to spend her hard earned money on something that tasted like 'watered-down Keebler elf piss.'"

Jacob made a face then nodded. Owen laughed. *You may not like her imagery, but you have to admit Grandma Campbell had a point.*

Owen signaled to Jacob when the time came to take the milk off the heat, so it was nice and warm but not scorched. Jacob mumbled something about not realizing you could scorch milk.

He stirred in the mix he'd made, and gave Jacob a spoon to sample it. Even though he didn't say anything, Owen could tell by the wide-eyed look the cocoa brought to his face that this was the best hot chocolate Jacob ever had.

Taking the ladle, Owen filled the mugs Jacob had arranged on two large trays. Carefully, they each grabbed a tray and headed back to surprise the other guests.

Everyone applauded Owen and Jacob when they tasted the cocoa. Owen grinned a little at the thought of being the hero of the evening. He was just trying to lighten things up around here. Okay, maybe if he was being honest, he was also trying to impress Jacob. *Jake*, he corrected himself. He liked the familiarity of the shortened name. If they were all spending the holiday together like one big, if slightly forced family, there was no need to stand on ceremony or formality.

He was so caught up in everyone enjoying themselves he hadn't even noticed Jake had slipped away. He looked up to see him returning from the front office with a bag of something that sounded like glasses clinking together. Jake set the bag on the table and began to pull out several mini bottles of peppermint schnapps.

"Ethel likes to keep these around in the winter." Jake shrugged. "She loves a mug of boozy hot chocolate in the evening."

"Perfect!" Owen wanted to give him a big kiss on the cheek, but he didn't think Jake would appreciate PDA in front of the entire group. He made a mental note to thank him for his thoughtfulness later.

*A*fter they'd finished the last cup of cocoa and sang along to a few of the carols from Mandy's playlist, the guests were starting to yawn. The excitement had worn out the kids, and the schnapps had made many of the adults feel warm and cozy enough to nod off. Soon they all started to wander off to bed, each of them stopping to thank Owen, Jacob, and even Mandy for making the day feel special.

Mandy disappeared before Jake had a chance to enlist her in the clean up effort, so Owen volunteered to help. They gathered up all of the mugs and took them back to the kitchen. Owen made quick work of the dishes while Jake took care of the trash and the bottles.

When he was finished, Owen headed back to the lobby to look for Jake. He found him sitting by the fireplace with two little bottles of schnapps.

"I found these left over," he said, following Owen's gaze. "Care to join me for a nightcap?"

Owen smiled warmly.

"Sounds lovely."

They both stared into the fireplace, sipping their little bottles of schnapps. A silence settled between them, comfortable at first, but awkwardness crept in after a few seconds.

"Um…" Jacob began, and Owen looked up to see his gaze wandering everywhere but Owen's face.

"What you did today…cheering everyone up, it helped me out a lot."

Owen wasn't really sure what to say to that, so he simply smiled and nodded.

"I mean, you really transformed this place." Jacob gestured to the lobby that now looked like a respectably festive setting for any number of B-list holiday movies.

"And the way you managed to get everyone working together," he continued. "Oh, and the hot chocolate, I mean, it was all just magical," he finished, blushing. Owen grinned at how the little flush of color made Jake look so alive.

"Call me a sap," Owen finally replied. "But I think everyone needs a little Christmas miracle now and then."

Owen noticed Jake roll his eyes.

"You're really not much of a festive kinda guy, huh?" Owen asked, trying to figure out where all this grinch energy came from. "Was Santa a little too generous with the coal shovel in your stocking?"

Jacob smiled, but it didn't really reach his eyes.

"I don't know about that, but...I don't know. Holidays were never particularly joyous at the Parker house."

Owen took a breath. He didn't really intend to open the Family Drama floodgates, but he'd started this, and now the tone of the conversation had turned too serious to diffuse with a joke or a flirtatious comment.

"Oh," Owen began, determined to tread with caution. "What, uh...what were they like?" He faltered. Not really sure what he was getting himself into.

Jacob was silent for long enough that Owen started to wonder if he wasn't going to respond.

"They were technically great," he said at last. "My parents would rent a ski chalet in the mountains. Christmas would be a weeklong celebration with a tree so tall you needed a ladder to place the star on top, more hot toddies than you could ever drink, and so many gifts. We sometimes stopped opening them about halfway through because we just wanted to play with the ones we'd already unwrapped."

"That sounds perfect," Owen cut in, trying to imagine what Christmas would be like if his family could afford a pristine holiday getaway in Aspen. "Sort of like a postcard."

"That's what my mother's carefully manicured family portrait for our Christmas card would like you to think." Jacob smiled ruefully. "But the postcard doesn't show how, as soon as the last gift was opened, my parents would send my brothers and me to our rooms to 'enjoy our new toys' while they went out skiing. It doesn't show how we wouldn't actually spend any time together, or how I have more memories of spending Christmas with my Rubik's cube than with my family."

"Oh, Jake, I'm sorry." Owen wanted to reach over and scoop him up in his arms and make everything okay.

"I came out after I turned eighteen," Jacob continued. "My parents said they loved me, and they certainly didn't cut me off or anything, but that year they booked their first holiday cruise. Ten days in the Caribbean, from December 22nd through New Year's. My older brothers were both either at college or celebrating with their own families at that point, so my parents took the opportunity to establish a new family tradition: putting an ocean between themselves and their gay son who they 'loved and accepted no matter what.'"

Jacob was staring deep into the fireplace, and the glow of the dying coals gave his eyes a haunted glint as he made air quotes around the last crushing words.

Owen's breath hitched. He never expected that so much pain lived just under the surface of all that sexy, stoic brooding.

"Jake, I-"

"So yeah," Jacob cut Owen off. "I have some baggage with Christmas. It's a little tough to feel merry and joyful when your childhood trauma tastes like peppermint and gingerbread."

Jacob made a dry little chuckle at his own joke, and Owen swore he could feel his own heart breaking a little. He knew he had to fix this. Somehow he had to give this man a Christmas filled with joy and warmth, and enough love to heal some of the wounds Jacob carried around with him. Even though they just met, Owen felt responsible for giving Jacob at least one Christmas worth remembering.

His mind whirred with possibilities, ways to use the limited resources available to him to piece together the best Christmas ever. He was so lost in plotting out how he could fix everything that he didn't hear Jacob announce he was heading off to bed. When he stood up, Owen snapped back to his chair by the fireplace, and the man who had just bared his soul to him.

"Let me help you blow out these candles," Owen said with a little too much enthusiasm. "We don't need a fire on top of a blizzard." He smiled at Jacob, and tried to convey in it all the warmth he was feeling for him in that moment.

"Okay, thanks."

They worked around the perimeter of the room, extinguishing the seemingly endless number of candles they'd lit in the lobby. Owen thought back to how special the evening was, and how he'd been able to coax Jake out of his shell. He smiled to himself, goofy and satisfied.

When they reached the front desk, they blew out all but two candles, so they could each have one to light the way back to their rooms. Jacob hesitated, and Owen was just about to say goodnight when he looked up and noticed the sprig of mistletoe Jake had hung up earlier. He didn't mention it while they were decorating because he didn't think he'd be able to resist pulling Jake in for a big, cheesy, fucking sexy kiss. He smiled as the impulse returned, but he didn't feel like resisting this time.

He took a half step closer to Jacob and gazed into his eyes, which flickered as they caught the candlelight. Jacob was frozen stock still, so Owen reached up to cup his cheek, soft and warm in his hand. They stared into each other's eyes one beat longer, then Owen leaned in and kissed Jacob, soft and tender. Jacob started to kiss back, rougher, pulsing with need, but Owen broke away, not wanting to rush things.

"Good night, Jacob Parker," he whispered. Then he grabbed his candle and headed toward his room before Jake could even say "you too."

CHAPTER 6

Jacob woke with a start, breathing ragged and dick achingly hard. He closed his eyes and allowed the memory of the dream he'd been having to wash over him.

He was back in the Elk Terrace lobby, flickering candlelight glinting off Owen's deep blue eyes. He stared into them, feeling warmth spread through his chest. Owen leaned in to kiss him, and he felt lighter than air. He kissed back, rough and passionate, but this time, Owen didn't pull away. This time Owen parted his lips and allowed Jacob's tongue to explore.

Jacob reached down to free his now straining erection from his flannel pants. He curled his fingers around his cock and gently began to stroke.

The warmth radiating throughout his body was now a searing heat, and Jacob knew he had to get his shirt off, or he wouldn't be able to stand it. His fingers fumbled to undo his buttons without breaking the kiss. Owen reached down to pull the shirt off from the hem, and between the two of them, they managed to send it cascading to the floor. Then Owen's hands were on his chest, running through the thick patch of hair, toying with the hard nubs of his nipples, and then gliding down to explore the lean muscles in his core.

Jacob was now stroking himself faster, his grip on his cock firmer than before. His heart was beating faster, and he could hear the blood rushing in his ears.

Before he knew it, Owen was shirtless too. Jacob surveyed his broad chest and the soft expanse of his stomach. He wanted to sink into that soft warmth and hide from all the stress of the blizzard, and the guests, and Mandy, and the holiday. He leaned down to lick one of Owen's taut, rosy nipples while his hands found Owen's belt and began to unfasten it.

Jacob was close now. He could feel the pressure building just below his navel. He needed release, ached for it.

He could hear Owen's soft moan as he pulled down his pants. He knew that he wanted to take Owen's cock in his mouth, but he didn't want to look away from his piercing gaze even for a second. Kneeling down low, he stared into Owen's deep blue eyes as he reached to tease the tip of his cock with his tongue.

"*Oh, Jake,*" *Owen said, softly, barely audible.* "*Jake. Jake!*"

Jacob came to the sound of Owen calling his name. His abdomen convulsed while he shot hot, thick ropes of cum all over the henley he'd been sleeping in the past few nights.

When he came to his senses, he realized that he could still hear Owen's voice calling his name, this time accompanied by a soft knock on the door.

"Jake, are you awake in there?" Owen followed his question with another soft knock.

Shit! I can't answer the door in a cum-stained shirt.

He looked around for something to change into, but his

bag wasn't in reach. A spike of panic at the thought of missing the opportunity to see Owen shot through him, and he decided just to pull his shirt off as he scrambled to answer the door.

"Owen? What's wrong?"

"Uh..." Owen stammered, but Jacob saw he was distracted by the sight of his bare chest.

Jacob's blush, deep and warm, spread over the exposed skin that captivated Owen's attention.

"Oh, nothing, I just..." Owen blinked a few times, dipping his head in embarrassment. "I just had an idea for how to cheer everyone up. Can I come in?"

"Um..." Jacob struggled to process the thoughts now swirling through his head.

He was embarrassed by the state Owen found him in, but the moment they shared last night, the intimacy of their conversation, not to mention the desire Owen apparently stirred in him, had him craving more. He wanted to be close to him, to share more about himself and to hear more about Owen, maybe even to touch...

"Sorry about the mess," Jacob said, rushing to collect the dirty clothes and *oh god* underwear that he'd left strewn around the floor.

"I didn't even notice," Owen reassured him. "I can come back, if you need a minute."

"No!" Jacob said, a bit too quickly. "I mean, what did you want to tell me?"

Jacob finally came across an undershirt that he'd worn the previous day, and pulled it on to hide from Owen's lingering gaze. He could have sworn he saw a hint of a frown flash across Owen's face when he noticed the shirt. Clearly he was going crazy.

"Well, it's Christmas Eve, and I just checked the news. The highway is still closed.."

Jacob sighed. He'd been too preoccupied to check, but he held out hope that the guests could leave today. Now that hope shattered under the weight of all the snow and the accompanying stress.

"So I figured that everyone would need some cheering up."

"Okay." Jacob was hesitant to agree to doing anything special for some of the guests, but Owen's enthusiastic smile melted through his resentment. "What did you have in mind?"

"Here, put this on," Owen said, tossing Jacob a ridiculously cheesy Christmas sweater. "It'll be a bit baggy on you, but you need to look festive if we're gonna pull this off."

Jacob stared at the sweater. The design was a reindeer with glittery fake fleece fur, actual jingle bells hanging from each antler point, and a shiny nose that lit up bright red and played the melody of "Rudolph the Red-Nosed Reindeer" when you pushed a button concealed in the sleeve. Jacob wouldn't be caught dead in it normally, but judging by everything he knew about Owen, he guessed that this might be his favorite Christmas sweater; at least it matched the color of the Santa hat he insisted on wearing every minute of the day. Jacob smiled at the thought as he pulled it over his head. It was about three sizes too big for him, but he could still reach the button in the sleeve, so he pushed it. Owen smiled as the little melody plinked away, and Jacob gave the jingle bells a little shake for emphasis.

"Come on," Owen instructed, grabbing Jacob's hand and leading him out into the hall.

Jacob hadn't had time to process the sudden contact when

he saw what Owen had prepared. Sitting on a repurposed housekeeping cart were two large carafes of the now famous Campbell family hot chocolate, along with a sizable platter of warm, sweet-smelling cinnamon rolls.

"Where did those come from?" Jacob asked, unable to disguise the note of incredulity in his voice.

Owen smiled, warm and mischievous.

"Grandma Campbell's homemade cinnamon rolls. They take a little extra time to make the dough, but you can't beat the authentic ooey-gooey, homemade goodness."

Jacob stared at him in disbelief.

"Are you possessed by the ghost of a 1950s domestic goddess?" he asked, vaguely expecting the person in front of him to tear off the Owen mask like a *Scooby Doo* villain to reveal that it had been Martha Stewart the whole time.

"Maybe by the *Spirit* of Christmas," Owen said, chuckling at his own joke.

Jacob rolled his eyes, but couldn't hold back a grin at the cheese factor.

"So, what Christmas song do you hate the least?"

"Uh... Why?" Jacob was instantly suspicious.

"Oh, no reason." Owen smiled coyly as he turned to push the cart down the hall. "We're just going caroling."

Jacob's stomach dropped. "We're doing *what*?" It was just after eight, and even the early risers he'd noticed yesterday seemed to be trying to sleep out the storm.

His pulse spiked with anxiety, but Owen was already knocking on the first guest's door and waving him over.

"Pick a song. Any song," Owen hurriedly whispered.

Jacob's heart beat even faster as he heard the person behind the door sliding open the chain lock.

The door opened, and his mind went blank. He opened his mouth and the first few bars of "God Rest Ye Merry

Gentlemen" fell out before he remembered he was even capable of making sound.

Owen looked over at him, smiling as he joined in.

Mr. Peterson of room 12 was initially flustered by the early morning interruption, but the dose of Christmas cheer, spurred on in no small way by Owen's hot chocolate and pastries, soon brought a smile to his face. He began to applaud as Owen and Jacob warbled out their last "tidings of comfort and joy," and Jacob smiled at the warm feeling slowly stirring in his heart.

At the next room, Mrs. Ramirez, room 11, Owen started in with "Deck the Halls." By the time they reached room 9, Mrs. Weisse and her son, Jacob was so focused on the warmth in his chest that he forgot to be anxious when Owen started "O, Little Town of Bethlehem."

By the time they reached the last room, they were a little drunk on the excitement of bringing smiles to so many faces. They were laughing, arms around each other's shoulders, as they bellowed out the last line of "We Wish You A Merry Christmas" to the small assembly of guests that had formed in the hall to enjoy the show. Some joined in the singing; others just stood back and smiled.

Jacob couldn't remember another time when he'd felt so alive and so comfortable in a group of relative strangers. He looked over to smile at Owen, only to find that Owen was already smiling at him.

"Merry Christmas," Owen whispered to him.

They took their bows, and the guests began shuffling toward their rooms. A few of them even stopped to praise Owen for his baking prowess. He grinned bashfully, and Jacob felt a new fondness for Owen that almost made the goofy sweaters, the decorating, the caroling, even the dream he'd had all make sense.

As the final guest finished congratulating them and trying to pry Owen's cinnamon roll recipe from him, even though he insisted that it was a Campbell family secret, Jacob noticed there was enough hot chocolate left for two mugs, and three cinnamon rolls.

Jacob was about to offer the third roll to Owen when he reached down and split it in half. Owen smiled sweetly at Jacob, and he felt the warmth in his chest increase by a degree or two. He smiled back, and they ate in silence.

~

The morning went smoothly after that. A couple of the guests took it upon themselves to make a proper breakfast for everyone, and one of the kids hooked her laptop up to the big TV in the lobby and was playing Christmas movies. After several people, including, much to Jacob's surprise, Owen, vetoed *A Christmas Story*, they settled on *Home Alone*.

"Only the first two," Owen insisted. "The other so-called sequels shouldn't even be mentioned."

All in all, despite a brief downturn when the morning news reported roads were to remain closed today, Owen's morning festivities had everyone in high spirits. It was a Christmas miracle, and Jacob wasn't about to question it.

When the movie finished, Owen caught Jacob's eye and gestured for Jacob to follow him down the hall toward the kitchen. Jacob stole a quick glance around the lobby to see if anyone was watching him, but everyone seemed absorbed in their own business. Jacob smiled to himself and made his way down the hall.

In the kitchen, Jacob saw Owen gathering flour, sugar, and Ethel's stash of chocolate chips which she hid inside a mostly empty box of baking soda so Mandy, and if he were being honest, Jacob, wouldn't eat them before she could bake her signature cookies.

"Have you ever made Christmas cookies before?" Owen asked him with a bright, excited smile.

"Not like this," Jacob replied, a note of amazement in his voice. "My mother would always buy the premade ones, the kind you just have to bake, with reindeer faces and Christmas trees on them."

Owen wrinkled his nose in disgust, and Jacob couldn't remember ever seeing someone have such a strong emotional reaction to cookies.

"Okay," Owen said in the voice of someone trying to explain a concept for the hundredth time to someone who just wasn't getting it. "Those aren't cookies. Those things aren't even wafers. They're like desiccated, sugary little hockey pucks."

"Oh, come on!" Jacob protested. "I thought you liked festive shit. Don't I get extra points for eating cookies with Rudolph's face on them?" He pushed the button in his sleeve and made the sweater play the tune to "Rudolph the Red-Nosed Reindeer" for emphasis.

"Hmmm," Owen said stroking his golden blond beard as if considering Jacob's offer. "Tell you what, I'll give you three extra points for Rudolph, and another two just for being cute, but that still puts you several hundred points in the negative for not knowing what an acceptable Christmas cookie is."

Jacob's breath hitched at the compliment.

"Well then, would the all-knowing judge of all things holiday ever deign to teach me the secret to 'real Christmas cookies?'" Jacob teased, suddenly more bold than normal.

The smile Owen flashed him was reason enough to try more of the confident sarcasm in the future.

They made enough cookie dough to feed an army: two batches of sugar cookie, one snickerdoodle, and one chocolate chip, which even though it wasn't technically holiday themed, Owen insisted that the archetypal homey feel of chocolate chip would go a long way with the guests. They joked and teased each other as they mixed and rolled out the dough, using Ethel's robust collection of holiday cookie cutters to make candy canes, stocking, trees, Santa hats, and even little elves.

While the first round of cookies was baking, Owen whipped up an honest-to-God Swiss buttercream.

"Let me guess," Jacob said. "Grandma Campbell's secret family buttercream recipe?"

"Nope." Owen grinned. "This one comes from America's grandmother: Martha Stewart." Owen held up his phone to show Jacob the recipe he found on Martha Stewart's website. Jacob smiled and rolled his eyes. Maybe Owen wasn't all-knowing after all. Even Jacob could look up and follow a recipe. In theory.

When the last two baking sheets went in the oven, Jacob finally worked up the courage to ask the question that had been on his mind all day.

"So what was it like?" he began. "Growing up in the Campbell household? You had me unpack all of my childhood baggage last night, so now the spotlight is on you."

Owen hesitated for a moment, and Jacob worried that his tone was somehow too forceful, too accusatory.

"I- I mean," he stammered. "If you don't mind talking about it."

"No, no." Owen waved off the idea. "It's fine. I'm just trying to figure out how to put it."

Owen was quiet for another moment, and Jacob was almost ready to tell him not to worry about it, and that he shouldn't have pried.

"It was good, but also hard," Owen began slowly. "My parents were very poor, still are in fact, so my sister and I didn't have a lot. Usually it wasn't a huge deal; my mom was a whiz at finding creative ways to pretend that poverty didn't exist. But it got a little hairy around the holidays."

Jacob was listening and nodding along with rapt attention. He tried not to smile at the idea of Little Owen, given the tone of what Adult Owen was sharing.

"My parents are kind of a rare breed for small-town Colorado. They somehow managed to navigate the typical working-class poor lifestyle without all of the religion and fundamentalism that runs rampant through everywhere west of Vale."

Jacob nodded. He knew what all the conservatism and religion could do to a family, particularly when one of the kids is gay. He scolded himself for feeling a pang of jealousy about Owen's upbringing, despite the relative privilege of his own.

"So around Christmas time, not only could we not afford the vacations, or the flashy presents, or even the big, tacky, inflatable lawn ornaments, but we also didn't do the whole midnight mass, nativity scene, first Christmas story part of the holiday either. In fact, my dad was very much of the opinion that if people were going to do the whole Christmas thing, they should at least be honest about it being all about Santa, selling expensive toys to bratty children, and keeping the ghosts of some obscure northern European solstice traditions alive for some reason. He always said, and I'm quoting directly here, 'the whole magic baby charade was just a waste of time and money.'"

A fit of laughter exploded out of Jacob with such force he was practically spasming. On one hand, he was surprised to hear such vehement anti-religious sentiment from any blue-collar small-towner. On the other, though, he couldn't help but laugh at the image of his mother's face if she could have heard the "magic baby" line. He imagined her turning redder than Owen's Santa hat.

When they had both calmed down a bit, as Jacob's reaction had set Owen off laughing as well, he continued his story.

"So anyway, we basically had to make our own Christmas celebrations from scratch."

"That's where the famous Campbell Family Traditions came from, then?"

"Mhmm," Owen replied, but his gaze was somewhere far away. "My grandma would bake enough to feed the whole town, we'd decorate with anything we could get our hands on or make ourselves, and somehow mom would find some kind of activity to keep our spirits up every day from Thanksgiving to New Year's. Over the years, we kept the ones we liked and built on them. Even after Grandma died, and I went away to college, and eventually to Denver for work, we kept the traditions alive. And now that my sister has her kids, there's another generation to enjoy them."

Owen smiled wistfully, and Jacob felt a tightness in his throat brought on by the emotion Owen's story conveyed.

"I guess that's why Christmas is so special to me," Owen concluded, snapping out of his reverie. "Because it's something that we built together, sometimes even out of nothing. It's a big part of what kept us going, even during times when we couldn't really afford anything else. And it's what kept us together, even after we all went our different ways."

Owen finished his story, looking Jacob in the eyes and giving him a little half smile that Jacob identified as bashful, vulnerable.

Jacob searched for something to say, but he couldn't think of any words that fit what he was feeling. Instead, he acted on the only thing that did come to mind.

Jacob stepped toward Owen and kissed him, firmly yet tenderly, hoping that he could convey how grateful he was that Owen shared that part of himself, how special he felt to be given a peek inside such a special memory, and how happy he was to be spending this holiday with him, even if it did break some traditions. He tried to project all of this through his kiss, hoping that somehow Owen could sense it.

Then, as if he could indeed hear the thoughts that Jacob was practically shouting in his mind, Owen kissed him back.

CHAPTER 7

Owen parted his lips and allowed Jacob's tongue to explore his own. The kiss caught him off guard. He didn't think that rambling monologue about how his family tried to make the best out of their scant circumstances was particularly romantic, but the tenderness in Jacob's lips said otherwise.

Jacob moaned softly, but it was enough to send a shockwave of desire through Owen, emboldening him. He reached up to knot his fingers through Jacob's hair with one hand and to wrap the other around his waist, pressing them together. At another, deeper moan from Jacob, Owen took control of the kiss, his desire an almost tangible heat between them.

Owen pressed them up against the kitchen wall, hoping to find a good angle to compensate for the three or four inches Jacob had on him. Jacob's body melted under Owen's touch, willing him to take control, to go further. Owen pressed one more kiss onto Jacob's mouth, their teeth knocking together with the force of it, the need, before moving to scatter quick, searing kisses across the sharp angle of his jaw and down onto his neck.

Owen stayed there for a moment, savoring the spicy-sweet musk of Jacob's cologne and drinking in the sounds of Jacob's hitched breath and small noises of pleasure like they were his only source of sustenance; he felt like he could live forever in those few brief seconds.

Jacob's hands were busy exploring all of the curves and lines of Owen's body, and Owen felt its enthusiastic response. Electricity shot through his body, lighting up his nerve endings like fireworks under Jacob's touch, and the rapid tightening in his pants conveyed his need for more contact, more friction, more heat.

Owen slipped his hand all the way down Jacob's firm stomach, down to palm the erection bulging under Jacob's jeans. Right when he thought nothing in the world was as important as loosening the belt and freeing Jacob's cock, the timer on the oven sounded. The cookies were ready, and *holy shit*, he'd almost went down on Jake right here in the kitchen, where anyone could see. Was he really that thirsty for it? *Apparently so*, Owen thought, mentally scolding himself.

Jacob snatched the oven mitts of the counter and bent to remove the two baking sheets.

"Come on," he said, voice husky and demanding, as he stepped toward the door.

Owen grabbed the two sheets of frosted sugar cookies and followed him. When they reached the lobby, Jacob placed the cookie trays on the front desk.

"Hey, everyone," he announced, his voice more assertive than it typically was with the guests. "Owen made Christmas cookies They're fantastic. Help yourselves. Owen, I need to speak to you in the office."

With that, he turned on his heel and marched into the

hotel office. Owen hoped the other guests didn't suspect anything from the few staccato sentences he barked at them. Still, the need building in Owen's belly pulled him toward the office like a magnet.

As soon as the door clicked shut, Jacob was there, pushing Owen back against it, enveloping his lower lip in a ferocious, hungry kiss. Then Jacob thrust his hips forward to grind their mounting erections together through the coarse fabric of their jeans. Owen released a sound of pleasure from a deep, desperate part of himself, which he hadn't accessed in several years. The desire pulsing through him was ravenous, urgent, primal.

Owen wasn't waiting any longer, wasn't holding back for fear that his need might be too strong, or that people may not like him for his looks, or his size, or his goofy enthusiasm. His desire was driving him forward, and it was fueled by the desire he found mirrored in Jacob's body.

He flipped them around so Jacob's back was pushed against the office door. He broke the kiss, and brought his attention to his clumsy, fumbling fingers as they both rushed to release their straining cocks. Once free, Owen wrapped a hand around both and began to stroke vigorously, pressing more kisses into Jacob's neck as he did so.

"O- Owen..." Jacob moaned. "Owen, oh my... fucking Christ."

Hearing Jacob moan his name like that sent jolts of pleasure straight to the heat that was building just below his navel. He was close, so very close, and Jacob was too, judging by the ragged breathing and quickening pulse, which Owen could feel on his tongue as he mouthed along under his jawline.

He quickened his pace, and right as the heat and pressure approached their apex, in that moment when time slows, when every second feels hours long, every nerve ending on fire, the door to the supply closet opened, and they heard a voice.

"By the way, Jake, we should think about- Oh my God!" the voice shrieked.

As they pushed off each other, scrambling to cover themselves, Owen looked to see Mandy scurrying back into the closet and slamming the door. *Shit! She must have been in here on her phone, hiding from the guests,* he thought. *Now she's seen everything.*

Owen looked to Jacob for a reaction, and he was turning a deep shade of red as a tide of embarrassment crashed over him.

"Oh my God, you guys, I'm sorry sorry, oh my God!" Mandy called from inside the closet. "I swear I wasn't being creepy, Jake! I just heard your voice, and... Oh my God, I'm sorry!"

"It's alright, Mandy," Jacob assured her in what Owen assumed was the most casual voice he could manage given the circumstances. "You can come out now. Everyone is...decent."

The closet door creaked open slowly, as if Mandy didn't quite believe Jake's assurance of modesty.

"I am so sorry, you guys. I did *not* mean to spoil your moment, I just-"

"You're alright, Mandy," Jacob cut her off with a wave. "What is it you wanted to say?"

"I just figured-" Mandy began, looking just as embarrassed and at least twice as red as Jacob had been a moment ago. "We should maybe think about what we're gonna do to feed the masses today. That's all," she finished weakly.

"Yeah," Jacob said, pinching the bridge of his nose and

squinting as the weight of reality crashed down on him again. "Don't worry about it, Man. I'll work something out."

Mandy rushed past them, headed toward the door and an escape from the awkwardness.

"Oh, and Mandy?" Jacob called after her as she reached for the doorknob. "Not a word to the guests? Or Ethel?"

"Absolutely! I mean, I think it's great, and you two should definitely-" She gestured vaguely between the two of them. "But these lips are sealed. Not to worry"

Mandy shut the door behind her, and Owen released a breath he didn't realize he was holding. It came out as a deep belly laugh. Jacob looked at him like he'd never seen a less appropriate reaction to anything in his life, which quickly dissolved into a slightly frantic laugh of his own.

"Oh, man!" Owen gasped between slowly subsiding convulsions of laughter. "I haven't been caught in the act like that since, I don't even know, high school, maybe? This really takes me back."

"I'm glad you're enjoying the visit from the Ghost of Handjobs Past, but you didn't just get caught with your cock out in front of the coworker you have to look in the eye every day," Jacob cried, but the concern in his voice was only half serious.

"Calm down, Mr. Hermit of the Hills." Owen smirked, rolling his eyes a little. "Interacting with other people isn't going to kill you. At least she got quite the eyeful." Owen gave Jacob's crotch a pointed look, and then smiled as the blush, which might have permanently stained his features at this point, deepened another shade or two.

Jacob dipped his head in embarrassment, but then smiled.

"Hermit of the Hills? Really?"

"Mmhmm," Owen mumbled, turning to leave.

"Where are you going?" Owen wondered if Jacob meant for it to sound so desperate.

"You heard the boss. Someone has to cobble together a Christmas dinner. Keep everyone busy for a few hours and I'll do my best."

CHAPTER 8

Jacob stared at the door Owen had just closed behind him. His mind swam with everything that had just happened. He felt like he's been in that office for both several weeks and only a few seconds. He tried to piece together the flood of emotions and sensation into a cohesive timeline. Seeing Owen like that, so hungry and exposed. Being able to kiss him, to touch him. Wow. Jacob felt a warmth stirring in the deep place behind his navel. The desire in Owen's eyes, the warmth of his hand as he caressed their erections. Jacob could feel his heart beat faster just remembering it.

And then, *Yikes!* Mandy. Jacob had to find her, had to apologize for getting down and dirty at work and for putting her in such an awkward position. But what was he going to say? *Hey, Man, sorry you saw my genitals. Please don't file a workplace harassment claim against me. Also, that was the hottest thing that's ever happened to me, and I've never felt this way about someone quite so fast before, so if you could please give me advice on how to ensure we bone down before the snow lets up and I never see him again?* Somehow that didn't inspire much confidence. Still, he had to say something. He also did really want to find some not-mortifying way to ask her for advice.

He found Mandy sitting at a table in the far corner of the breakfast nook, munching on some of Owen's cookies and flipping through an issue of *Vanity Fair* no less than four months old. Jacob cleared his throat.

"Uh, Mandy," he began timidly. "Can we talk for a second?"

She nodded and looked up from her magazine as Jacob sat down opposite her.

"I am so sorry, Jake. I didn't mean to-" Mandy began, keeping her voice just above a whisper.

"No, Mandy, stop," Jacob cut her off. "*I'm* the one who's sorry. I shouldn't have-" He gestured vaguely. "At work of all places."

Jacob pinched the bridge of his nose. His own stupidity and indiscretion were stirring up a migraine.

"I just never meant for you to have to see any of that, and I should have at least taken it to my room. I know we have the whole 'no fraternizing with guests' rule, and I should have taken that more seriously, and I'm just really sorry."

"Whoa, whoa, whoa!" Mandy said, throwing up her hands in mock surrender. "Let's pull the brakes on that crazy train. You didn't do anything wrong."

"No! You deserve better than-"

"Jake, I'm a big girl," Mandy said, reaching up to cover his mouth. "I'm just fine. Besides, I kinda expected you two to get it on eventually; you've been giving each other bedroom eyes since he walked through the door."

"You thought- We've been- *What?*" Jacob stammered, thoroughly exasperated.

"Oh, honey. You really can be the most clueless queen at the party."

Jacob looked aghast.

"Let me break it down for you," Mandy mercifully kept her voice down to an enthusiastic stage whisper so none of the guests had VIP access to his personal life. "When he walked in you practically started drooling, tripping over your words and honest-to-God fidgeting. Very attractive, by the way."

He shot her a dirty look.

"Anyway," she went on, smirking at how she got under his skin. "He definitely noticed. The scruffy, burly, mountain man thing must have really worked for him because he was practically preening himself as you were checking him in. I honestly expected one of you to vault over the desk and go at it right then and there."

"How did you see all of this? Where were you?" Jacob suddenly felt a bit violated, like he was fourteen and somehow his diary was on display for the whole world to see.

"Watching the security cam feed," Mandy answered like it was the most obvious, logical conclusion in the world. "Hating the snow, contemplating ending it all if even one more guest walked through the doors, you know. The usual."

Jacob tried unsuccessfully to stifle a smile at Mandy's performative misanthropy.

"And leave me here to deal with the blizzard alone?" Jacob joked warmly now. "That's a one-way ticket to the Bad Place for sure."

"Look around, Jakey boy," Mandy grinned. "We're already here."

They both laughed at the absurdity and pent-up stress of the past few days, and Jacob realized that everything would be okay between them.

"You should totally go for it, by the way," Mandy said after the laughter died down and silence settled for a beat or two. "It would be totally hot, and Christ knows you could use a good lay. You're overdue."

Jacob wanted to fight back against Mandy's cutting observation, but he couldn't pretend she wasn't right. It *had* been a while, and if the little sample in the office was anything to go by, it would indeed be really fucking hot. But it was more than that, he realized. He liked spending time with Owen, with or without the heat, and the kissing, and the groping. He liked baking cookies, and hearing about the famous Campbell Family Christmases. He especially liked that he was still draped in Owen's dorky Rudolph sweater, so much so that the thought of him packing it away and driving off with it sent a spike of panic through Jacob's chest.

"I just...I want to get to know him, Mandy," Jacob said, trying to convey all of these new feelings, searching her face for some kind of answer. "I want to spend time with him, and learn what his life is like outside of this snowbound holiday hell."

"Damn, broski," Mandy said, placing a consoling hand on his shoulder. "You're in deep. Have you told him any of this?"

"Well...no," Jacob deflated, feeling like the world's biggest idiot.

"Why the fuck not?" Mandy demanded, raising her voice for the first time. "Did spending all that time silently brooding make you forget how to use your words?" Jacob bristled, but Mandy continued on full speed ahead. "The dude is nice, and cute, and apparently a regular down-home Betty Crocker, but I seriously doubt he's psychic. Don't wait around for him to read your mind. Use the balls that I can now visually confirm you have, and tell the man you want to date, or whatever."

Jacob's face turned white at Mandy's reference to his actual balls and at the thought of confessing to Owen all of the feelings that had begun to develop during their brief time together. Mandy might have been on to something, but he wasn't sure he had the courage to put himself out there like that. On the other hand, he wasn't sure he had the strength to watch him drive away, out of his life forever, either.

Jacob rubbed his eyes, searching for clarity, and a small, distressed groan escaped from the back of his throat.

"For the record," Mandy said, her tone softening with compassion. "I think you'd be an idiot not to go for it, and I would shame you mercilessly for letting him slip through your fingers, but it's your choice."

Jacob nodded, ruefully.

"But whatever you decide," Mandy's tone snapped back to her usual combination of sarcasm and apathy. "It'll have to wait. Lover boy gave us a job to do, so let's go distract the hostages."

Jacob shot her a questioning look.

"What?" Mandy asked with the worst impression of sincerity Jacob had ever heard. "I can respect your privacy and listen at keyholes at the same time. I'm very talented."

With that, Mandy slunk off to the lobby, leaving Jacob to wonder if it were possible to pop a blood vessel from rolling his eyes so hard.

~

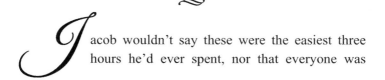acob wouldn't say these were the easiest three hours he'd ever spent, nor that everyone was

having the best time. But between sending the kids on makeshift scavenger hunts through the hotel for pillow mint rewards, and watching *The Muppet Christmas Carol* and *Miracle on 34th Street*, the 90s version with child acting prodigy and international bisexual icon Mara Wilson, not the slightly depressing, black-and-white version from the 40s, Jacob thought he did an okay job keeping everyone busy. Mandy was surprisingly helpful, and while Jacob knew better than to question her lightening the load for once, he couldn't help but think she somehow viewed this as her contribution toward getting him and Owen together. The idea was both annoying and sweet.

The kids were losing patience with the endless rounds of hide-and-seek and capture the flag, and Jacob wasn't looking forward to trying to convince everyone to sit through a third movie in a row. His plan to keep everyone busy was rapidly taking on water, and he wished Owen were here to work some more Christmas magic to keep everyone docile. But Owen had tasked him with keeping everyone happy precisely because he couldn't be there, and Jacob wasn't about to let him down. He put on *The Santa Clause* for the kids, and fished out a few decks of cards from an end table drawer. He was just about to challenge the adults to a poker tournament when Owen strode victoriously into the lobby. Jacob almost collapsed in relief.

"Is everything ready?" Jacob asked, frantically.

"Get everyone set up in the dining room and tell Mandy to throw on some music," Owen said, winking at him.

"Alright, folks," Owen announced to the room. "I'll need a couple of volunteers to help with dinner. Mrs. Ford, could I persuade you?"

"Of course!" she replied. "Anything you need, Owen."

Mrs. Ford and a couple of others followed Owen back into the kitchen, and Jacob was finally able to catch his breath.

He shepherded the guests into the dining room, taking care to group all of the kids together at their own table, despite heated protest from the oldest two. Mandy found a playlist of surprisingly tasteful orchestral carols, while Mrs. King led the charge to decorate with leftover candles. The anticipation was nearing its boiling point when Owen and his entourage of volunteers entered with an unbelievable array of delicious-looking dishes. There were three roasted chickens, a very traditional-looking stuffing, every frozen vegetable that Jacob was able to find at the market two days before, enough mashed potatoes to feed all of central Colorado, three whole pies, an entire tray of Grandma Campbell's famous cookies, and a very aromatic bread pudding, which, upon closer inspection, seemed to be made of chopped up bagels from the hotel pantry.

Jacob wasn't sure where Owen even got some of these ingredients. He must have brought back a better haul from the market than he'd realized, but everything that happened prior to almost hooking up in the office was kind of a blur. Admittedly, he didn't spend too much time in the kitchen, but this meal rivaled Ethel's best work. He looked up at Owen with the most incredulous grin he could manage, earning him another wink. Then Owen brought out his *pièce de résistance*: half a dozen pitchers of delicious eggnog with a heavy pour of rich, dark rum.

Somehow, despite tremendous limitations, Owen's Christmas feast managed to feed everyone to bursting, and his insistence on everyone sharing their favorite Christmas memories sated the homesickness and need for festivity.

Jacob was sipping his fourth glass of the potent eggnog, and had just finished recounting the year he and his brothers built two enormous snow forts and waged an all-out snowball war until dinner. Part of him never wanted the meal to end. Another, more demanding part was aching for the guests to leave so he could be alone with Owen.

CHAPTER 9

Dinner was winding down, and as Owen watched the guests slowly trickle away to their rooms, the buzz of anticipation began to fill the parts in his chest where joy and contentment had recently occupied. Some of the guests offered to help clean up and Owen did his best to rush through the process with them. He needed to be alone with Jacob; the space between them was driving him crazy.

When the last of the dishes were dried and stored in the cupboards, the volunteers bid each other goodnight, thanking Owen for his hard work and praising his talent. Owen felt a gleam of pride and appreciation at their praise, but at the moment, he thought the best way they could thank him was by shoving off. Finally, the last goodnight was said, the last refrain of praise came to a close and Owen had to restrain himself from sprinting to the dining room.

He tried to remain very casual as he entered, blowing out a few candles, and sliding a stray chair into place. Dismissing the idea of acting surprised that Jacob was still there as far too middle school, he instead opted for the direct approach, sitting across from Jacob at the table they'd shared that evening.

"Well, that went better than I expected," Owen said, breaking the tense silence.

Jacob gave him a curious sort of look and shook his head slightly.

"What?" Owen asked timidly.

"Who even *are* you?" Jacob asked, his tone as suspicious as his expression.

Owen didn't know how to answer that, but Jacob didn't give him much of a chance anyway.

"I mean, you just show up here one night with your dorky sweaters, and your stupid, gorgeous eyes and you somehow manage to single-handedly transform every holiday traveler's worst nightmare, not to mention my personal circle of hell, into an honest-to-God Hallmark movie? Oh and you happen to also be absurdly hot, kind to a fault, and maybe the best kisser I've ever met."

Owen's face was on fire. The eggnog must have been stronger than he realized to bring all this on.

"So I want to know where the fuck you even came from, because ever since I woke up this morning from a dream about going down on you, all I've wanted to do was throw you down on a bed and rip your clothes off with my teeth. How do you even-"

Owen leaned across the table to stop Jacob's rambling with a hot, desperate kiss.

"Sounds like a plan to me," he said, practically pulling Jacob out of the chair and pressing their lips together with such enthusiasm that they knocked teeth.

Jacob moaned deep in his throat, and the sound sent a shockwave of desire coursing through Owen. He was ready to get naked and start reenacting the finer points of Jacob's dream right then and there, but he remembered how embarrassed he'd been when they got caught earlier that day. He didn't want to put Jake in that position again.

Owen broke the kiss, looking into Jacob's eyes to see his pupils blown wide with arousal.

"My room. Now," he ordered and Jacob nodded, out of breath.

They made their way to the bedroom, stopping each other with fervent kisses several times along the way. They tried to be as quiet as possible to avoid drawing attention from the others, but Owen knew they couldn't restrain themselves for much longer. He fumbled with his key in his rush to get them inside, but at last the door was closed and all bets were off.

Owen locked the door; they weren't about to be interrupted this time. As soon as he slid the chain into position, Jacob's lips were on his again, his tongue massaging Owen's gently, but with an urgency that made Owen weak in the knees.

Jacob tugged on the hem of Owen's sweater and Owen pushed the small, insecure voice that sometimes told him to feel ashamed about his body thoroughly out of his mind. The desire between them burned like a palpable flame and if the already impressive bulge growing under Jacob's jeans was anything to go by, his size or shape wasn't going to be a problem for either of them.

Owen lifted his arms over his head to help Jacob remove the sweater and long-sleeved undershirt, breaking their kiss only to pass them over his head. Jacob brought the sweater to his nose and inhaled deeply. His breath came out in a low moan as he tossed the sweater aside, and Owen felt his jeans becoming uncomfortably tight.

Jacob took a moment to admire his body, from the soft, golden curls that spread across his chest, to the smooth curve of his stomach. Owen dropped his gaze, attempting to minimize the force of Jacob's appraisal. The initial embarrassment of being closely observed faded, however, when Jacob lifted his chin to recapture his mouth in a kiss. For a brief moment, Owen saw the hunger in Jacob's eyes, and the jolt of desire it sent through his whole body left him aching for Jacob to have his way with him.

True to his word, Jacob slowly backed Owen up to the edge of the bed, and with a careful yet firm push, sent him falling backward onto the duvet. Jacob climbed on top of Owen, positioning himself just right so his perfect, firm, tragically still clothed ass was straddling his cock, driving him wild. Jacob remained there for several seconds, taking time to alternate between scattering soft, tantalizing kisses down Owen's neck, and returning to his mouth, deep and hungry. Owen began to impatiently wonder if this was as far as they were going to go when Jacob's kisses suddenly crept downward. He kissed down Owen's neck, occasionally darting out his warm, wet tongue to massage the places where he sucked too enthusiastically. Owen smiled to himself, thinking of how, at twenty-six, he was going to have to explain why he showed up to Christmas dinner covered in goddamn hickeys. He chuckled softly at the thought.

Jacob looked up from teasing Owen's firm, taut nipple with a questioning look on his face. Owen simply smiled and reached up to guide his head back down, savoring the sparks of pleasure that jolted across his chest at Jacob's attentions.

Owen's moan resonated throughout his core, which must have signaled Jacob to go even further, because he shimmied down off of Owen's hips, kissing and licking his way down his stomach as his hands made quick work of Owen's Santa's Workshop belt buckle and the button of his waistband. Then his pants were sliding down, along with his underwear, and he lifted his hips off the bed to grant Jacob easier access.

Owen's breath rushed out of his lungs when Jacob's rough, firm hand grasped his cock, only to be drawn back in with a sharp gasp as he took the head into his mouth. He gently sucked on the head while his tongue fluttered back and forth, teasing the underside and very sensitive tip. Owen knotted his fingers in the duvet, desperately trying to restrain himself from bucking his hips up and forcing himself further into Jacob's throat.

Jacob pulled off Owen's cock with an obscene pop and Owen had to bite back a noise of frustration at the loss of the warmth and the suction. His complaints fell away as Jacob kissed down the side of Owen's shaft and then licked a single thick, perfectly wet stripe up the underside of it. Jacob returned the cock to his mouth, and Owen moaned in earnest as he felt his entire length slide past Jacob's perfect lips and back into his throat.

"Oh, Jake," Owen cried out breathlessly.

Jacob moaned around Owen's cock and he felt the vibration all the way down his dick and into his balls. Owen couldn't help bucking his hips this time, which made Jacob gag and pull off him.

"Shit! I'm sorry." Owen's voice rose with concern.

"Owen," Jacob sighed, seemingly unbothered. "Jesus Christ! Do that again."

Jacob slid his cock back into his mouth and Owen bucked up gently, experimentally. Jacob gagged slightly, but then hummed with pleasure. He reached up to grab Owen's hand and placed it on the back of his own head, encouraging him to pull his head down even further onto his cock. Emboldened by Jacob's enthusiasm, Owen fucked his mouth until he pulled away, red-faced and panting.

"I need you inside me," Jacob almost pleaded. Owen couldn't decide if he was more disappointed by the absence of Jacob's mouth on his cock or more desperate to fuck his tight little ass.

"Strip," Owen commanded.

Jacob pulled off the sweater he'd been wearing since that morning, and unbuttoned the flannel underneath so quickly that Owen wondered how he managed not to rip the buttons off entirely.

Owen sat up and pulled Jacob in close enough to lick a long stripe from his navel, up past the soft patch of hair that dusted the low ridges of his firm abs, all the way to one of his hard nipples, which he sucked between his lips and released with a sharp smack of a kiss.

"Lose these too," Owen ordered, impatiently tugging on Jacob's belt loops.

Jacob unfastened his jeans, reaching in to pull a condom and a small bottle of lube out of his pocket before sending them cascading to the floor. When Owen shot a disbelieving look at the supplies, Jacob shrugged.

"Picked some up at the gas station yesterday," he explained. "Just in case."

"Well, that was very presumptuous of you," Owen mock-chided. "But I'd hate to see them go to waste," he concluded with a mischievous smile.

Jacob peeled the foil wrapper off the condom, careful not to damage the delicate latex. Then he did something Owen had never seen before, despite his relatively prolific experience. He placed the condom between his lips and bent down to take Owen's cock in his mouth again, using his tongue to guide it down the whole length of the shaft.

"That was the hottest thing I've ever seen!" Owen said as Jacob rose up and climbed onto the bed on his knees.

"That's not the only trick up my sleeve," Jacob teased, and Owen's dick twitched as he imagined what else Jacob could show him. But that would have to wait. Right now, their need was too great, the heat between them too strong for any more exploration. They needed each other, needed to fuck.

Jacob popped open the bottle of lube and squeezed a generous amount into his hand, reaching back to slick Owen's cock and massaging the excess into his already hungry hole.

Owen licked his lips in anticipation, determined to remain completely still as Jacob lowered himself onto his dick. He wanted Jacob to feel comfortable, to move at his own pace… at first anyway. Finally, Owen felt the tip of his cock push up against the tight ring of muscle, slick with lube. Owen held his breath for one impossibly long second, and then the tip of his cock was pushing past the resistance into the warm, silky tightness.

Jacob groaned as his body adjusted to the intrusion, and Owen had to fight against every muscle and cell of his body not to rush full speed ahead. He wanted Jacob to be comfortable, to enjoy this moment as much as he was. He wanted to move at Jacob's speed, even if that meant waiting for what felt like an eternity.

Finally, finally, Jacob started to slide down his length. Slowly, inch by inch, Owen's cock was enveloped in the heat of Jacob's ass. Then, just when Owen thought he couldn't bear it any longer, Jacob began to move, slowly at first, halfway up the shaft, and then down again, taking his time. Owen relaxed into the bed, savoring the sensation.

"Oh, Jake…" Owen whispered, eliciting another long, low moan from him.

Jacob started to move faster, riding him in earnest now, and Owen's body undulated with the steady rhythm.

"Holy fuck, Owen!" Jacob cried out. "Your dick is perfect."

"Mmm," Owen hummed contentedly. He reached up to grasp Jacob's fully erect cock, stroking it in time with the pace of his ass.

"You're not so bad, yourself," Owen ribbed, teasing his sensitive tip with his thumb. Jacob choked out a breathy laugh and quickened his pace.

"In fact," Owen said, beginning to thrust up into Jacob to punctuate his thought. "I want to see how this bad boy feels inside me."

"I- Are you sure?" Jacob stammered out.

"Sure am," Owen insisted, his voice becoming gravelly with lust. "Want me to show you how we take dick where I come from?"

"Fuck, yes!" Jacob almost shouted as Owen gave a particularly sharp thrust.

"Get up," he ordered, slapping Jacob's ass and eliciting a moan to rival the resounding *smack*.

Jacob eased off of him and onto his feet. He reached a hand out to help Owen off the bed. Owen pulled off the condom and sank to his knees in front of Jacob. He gave Jacob's cock a few preliminary strokes, looking up to meet his gaze with a wicked grin before swallowing his entire cock in a single go. He sucked, slow and hard, up the whole length of Jacob's shaft, taking a moment to swirl his tongue around the head, licking up the salty precum that leaked from the tip.

"Jesus fuck, man!" Jacob gasped as Owen pulled off him.

"You're not the only one with tricks."

Owen reached into his bag for his bathroom bag and retrieved the condom and packet of lube he stored there.

"I never go anywhere without one," he said, tearing it open. He spit on Jacob's dick to wet it and rolled the condom on with three tantalizing strokes, slicking on the lube with a fourth.

"How do you want me?" Owen asked, standing up. Jacob's breath came out rough and ragged, and Owen swore he could detect a hint of a growl in it. Suddenly, Jacob spun him around to face the bed and shoved him down onto his elbows.

Apparently being a little forceful is one of his famous tricks, Owen thought, but he wasn't about to object. Jacob raked his fingers down his back, coming to rest on his ass, which he kneaded before spreading his cheeks wide and spitting on his hole. Owen let loose a desperate groan as the ring of muscle twitched then opened slightly in anticipation.

"Fuck, Jake! Put it inside me. Need to feel you."

"You sure you're ready?" Jacob asked sweetly and timidly, which only made Owen's need grow more insistent.

"I've been waiting for this all day. I'm ready," Owen assured him, the urgency in his voice cutting through all of Jacob's reservations.

Clearly Jacob needed no more encouragement because he lined his dick up with the angle of Owen's hole and with no further comment pressed his entire length inside. Owen moaned long and low again as Jacob filled him completely, stretching him wide, dick pulsing with desire. He pulled almost all the way out, leaving only the tip inside, before pushing all the way back in. He did this a few more times, and while Owen loved the sweet agony of the slow, luxurious thrusts, he silently begged Jacob to kick it into high gear.

As if on cue, Jacob began to accelerate his tempo, soon matching, then outstripping the pace with which he rode Owen's cock. Owen arched his back and rocked into Jacob on the in-thrusts, tilting his hips so that his every move brushed against Owen's prostate, each time sparking a fire which consumed him from the inside out.

"Jake... Right there... Fuck me harder."

Somehow, Jacob accelerated his already frenetic pace, adjusting his angle once more to slam directly into Owen's spot. Owen's moans came out in a refrain of pleasure, and Jacob provided a deep, steady harmony with his own. Owen knew he couldn't hold out much longer against the pro-level fucking Jacob had been hiding behind all that flannel and surliness. He spit in his hand and reached down to stroke his own cock, not quite able to match Jacob's rhythm, but giving it his best shot.

It seemed like no time at all had passed since Owen began stroking himself, but all at once he was coming, hot and thick, all over the duvet. He could feel his ass tightening around Jacob's cock with each spurt of his orgasm, and the wild, strangled noises coming from behind him only pushed him further into pleasure. Almost immediately, Owen felt Jacob's cock begin to pulse inside of him, and before he had a chance to brace himself, Jacob had pulled all the way out, torn off the condom, and shot his load all over Owen's back. He could feel the warm, wet ribbons of cum hitting his body, sending shockwaves through him that he felt all the way in his fingertips.

When he was finished, Jacob leaned down over him and pressed their bodies together, kissing behind Owen's ear and whispering incomprehensible phrases through his ragged panting breaths.

"...So fucking beautiful...," Owen managed to catch. "... Do this every day..." Owen reached to cup Jacob's head, stroking the back of his neck with the soft pad of his thumb.

When his breathing returned to normal, Jacob pushed off Owen and headed in the direction of the bathroom. He returned a moment later with a clean hand towel and wiped them dry. Once he had cleaned the cum from his own stomach, he gently wiped down Owen's back, pressing kisses into every place he cleansed. Owen couldn't remember ever being pampered so much after getting bent over and pounded within an inch of his life. Jacob gingerly turned him over, wiping his own cum from his stomach and thighs. Owen braced himself for the shock of the rough towel against his postorgasm-tender dick, but instead, Jacob bent down and took Owen's softening cock into his mouth and sucked it clean in one smooth, delicious motion.

"Oh my God, Jake," Owen said, the lust that had colored his voice only moments ago replaced by something softer, but just as warm. "That was the best fuck I've ever had." He pulled Jacob in for a long, lazy kiss, trying to convey through it the tenderness that had moved into his chest.

Jacob pulled away.

"You're not so bad, yourself," he jokingly repeated Owen's words, breaking into the widest, brightest smile Owen had seen from him yet, then scooping him up in a kiss before he could scold him for killing the mood.

Owen slid back to the head of the bed and burrowed under the covers. He reached for Jacob to join him and they kissed deeply again. In the stillness, they heard the old grandfather clock in the lobby chime midnight. They ushered in the holiday in each other's arms.

"Merry Christmas, Owen."

"Merry Christmas, Jake."

With that, Jacob turned to face the opposite wall, curled his back as closely as he could around Owen's body, and cuddled into the warmth of his arms. Owen brushed a single, featherlight kiss onto his neck, and without another thought, they drifted asleep together.

CHAPTER 10

Jacob awoke to the sound of snoring. It was hot. Owen was apparently a human furnace, and his arm almost scorched the skin where it wrapped around Jacob's waist. He could feel Owen's erection stabbing into his lower back. A small swell of pride arose in his chest at being able to make a man hard even in his sleep. He considered waking Owen up with a lazy morning blowjob, but a feeling of dread began to gnaw at the pit of his stomach. Somehow, he could feel their little snowbound fantasy rapidly coming to an end.

He clenched his ass experimentally; as he expected, he felt the familiar soreness from bottoming after a long dry spell, made even worse by the impressive combination of Owen's size and enthusiasm. He didn't expect someone so mild-mannered and gentle to be so…opposite in bed. Jacob was used to being the rough one. When your hookup pool consisted of cock-hungry, twenty-something trustfunder twinks and middle-aged, devoutly-Christian investment bankers who liked to be dominated, you don't get many chances to practice your bottoming skills. He was happy to discover Owen was more than capable of giving just as well as he received.

Warmth was beginning to build deep behind his navel as he recalled the heat and passion between them last night. He wanted to reach down and encourage the growing tightness in his briefs, but the nagging sense of inevitable ending ate away at his desire. He felt vulnerable, like every second that ticked severed another thread from their already delicate connection. In that moment, he realized he felt more than just attraction for Owen. If this were any other situation, he would say that there was potential to develop this connection into something real. *Fuck.* He couldn't let himself fall down that rabbit hole. Their time together was a weekend fling made possible by the absurdity of extraordinary circumstances. Imagining it as anything else was a recipe for disaster that would impress even old Grandma Campbell.

Still, Owen was soft and warm against him, and the world outside of his embrace seemed so distant and cold. Jacob turned to face him. He looked so peaceful, like all the stress and disappointment from not seeing his family all week, from missing the traditions, from being unable to see the smiles on his nephews' faces, had stolen away in the night as they slept in each other's arms. The sun, now filling the room with a soft golden light as the morning climbed above the trees, lit up Owen's sleep-rumpled blond hair like a fiery halo. He looked so beautiful, Jacob couldn't resist reaching out to touch him. He cupped Owen's cheek, and almost immediately, his breathing hitched and his eyes fluttered open.

"Good morning," Owen said with a gentle smile, his voice still rough from sleep.

"Merry Christmas," Jacob returned, moving his hand up

to run through Owen's hair, smoothing down the awkward spikes you get from going to sleep with product still in.

Owen leaned in to kiss him, and Jacob melted into it, eagerly parting his lips to allow his tongue inside.

"I had fun last night," Owen said, breaking the kiss and looking directly into Jacob's eyes.

"Yeah," he almost sighed, his tone embarrassingly dreamy, causing a hint of color to rush to his cheeks. "I mean, me too," he added, clearing his throat and trying to shake the affectionate daze from his face.

Owen chuckled.

"I know I'm good, but it's been a while since I've rendered anyone speechless."

Jacob gently shoved his shoulder and screwed up his face in a look of mock disdain.

"Don't flatter yourself," Jacob teased, even as he pulled Owen in for another long, deep kiss.

Jacob felt Owen's hand smooth over his chest, stopping to tweak a stiffening nipple before sliding past his ribs to explore further down. Only a moment ago, Jacob had been glad that the duvet was hiding the evidence of exactly how good he thought Owen was, but he knew if this went any further, his cover would surely be blown. *Not that I'd object too strongly to some blowing right now*, he thought, and his dick gave an interested twitch at the wordplay.

Owen's hand found the curve of Jacob's ass, and as he shifted to press their upper bodies together, his hand slipped under the waistband of Jacob's underwear to cup his cheek. Jacob's cock pulsed with arousal, and Owen must have noticed the material tightening, because he pulled his hand out and lightly brushed against Jacob's erection.

"Mmmmmm," Owen hummed, grasping the now impossibly hard dick. "Talk about rendering someone speechless. I could barely catch my breath with this big boy inside me." Owen punctuated the sentence with a firm but playful squeeze.

"We could go for round two," Jacob said, his eyes dark and hungry. "See if any words come to you this time."

Owen leaned over him, pressing the back of his head against the pillow as he caught his mouth in a deep, lust-filled kiss. He gave Jacob's cock a few teasing tugs, and Jacob moaned into their still joined mouths. Jacob was about to ask if Owen had any more condoms in his travel case when he suddenly broke away.

"But that will have to wait," Owen said, tossing off the blankets and stepping out of bed. He had switched gears so thoroughly that no one would even guess he'd spent the past five minutes getting them both more hot and bothered than Jacob could remember being at any point in his adult life. Owen grabbed his toiletry bag and headed to the bathroom, closing the door before Jacob could even process what just happened.

"Cocktease!" he yelled toward the door, and he was sure he heard laughing right before the sound of the faucet obscured any other noise coming from the room.

Jacob lay back on the bed. He tried to be very present, deciding that if their time together really was coming to an end in a day or two, they could still make the most of what they had. His plan was to get Owen back in bed when he was finished with his morning routine; after that, everything would fall into place. To that end, he jumped up, straightened out the bed, and stripped off his underwear. Even though he never really saw himself as the seductive type, he wanted to give it his best shot. He splayed himself out on the center of the bed, and lazily stroked his still very hard cock, lingering in the excitement and anticipation.

Right when he was certain his plan would work, that Owen would open the door, see him there, and they would spend the rest of the day tangled up in each other, he heard the shower turn on and his confidence deflated. *He really was serious,* Jacob thought, disappointment seeping into his limbs and softening his dick. *He actually wants to start the day, business as usual.* Jacob covered his head with a pillow and groaned in frustration, then he got up and began dressing. He put on his long johns, jeans, and undershirt, but decided to leave the Christmas sweater with its proper owner. No sense in hanging onto it, like Owen was his boyfriend or something.

He moved to straighten up the room just to keep his hands busy. He disposed of the used condoms and wrappers, changed the liner in the wastebasket, set some coffee to brew in the little machine on the credenza, and began stripping the bed and remaking it with new linens from the little cupboard by the door. The shower turned off right as the coffee finished brewing. He poured them both a cup and waited. Suddenly, he heard an excited whooping coming from the bathroom, making him jump and spilling hot coffee all over his hand. Owen burst through the door in nothing but a towel, holding his phone and smiling so wide Jacob was sure he could count all of his teeth.

"Oh my God, Jake!" Owen rushed to him, shoving his phone into his face before he could even enjoy the sight of post-shower Owen. "It's another real-life Christmas miracle!"

He turned up the volume on his phone, and Jacob sat there in mild shock as the local weather report announced the snow had broken during the night and plows had already cleared most of I-70 between Denver and Grand Junction.

"We'll all be able to make it home for Christmas dinner!"

Owen kissed him on the cheek and he managed to force a smile. He didn't know what to say. Feeling disappointed was incredibly selfish, given how much he knew spending Christmas with family meant to Owen, but this was all happening too soon. They only had one night together, and now he had to get excited about the fucking snow plows tearing them apart? *Merry fucking Christmas*, he thought, struggling to keep the bitterness off his face.

"That's so great, Owen," he said, desperately trying to inject some positivity into his voice. "I should go let everyone know. Spread the holiday cheer."

With that, he stood, scooped up the pile of soiled linens, and headed for the door. Not wanting to leave on a sour note, or betray any of the unhappiness that was weighing down his chest, crushing him, he turned and smiled as warmly as he could.

"Come and find me in the lobby before you leave," he said, surprised that his voice managed to sound completely normal, like nothing had changed. "I'll put out a breakfast spread of whatever we have left. Oh, and I made you some coffee." He nodded toward the paper cup by the coffee maker before turning to leave, closing the door behind him.

CHAPTER 11

Owen winced as the bedroom door closed a little harder than he expected. *What was* that *about?* He thought everything was going great between them. Spending practically every second together for the past three days, waking up in each other's arms, not to mention what happened last night, all signs pointed toward a successful start to…whatever this was. *Then why was he practically tripping over himself to get away from me?* Owen wondered if he did something wrong. Maybe Jacob felt rejected because he didn't want to get off this morning? He thought they had something more than just sex. Jacob didn't even seem like one of those strictly physical kind of guys. Well, whatever it was, he was running out of time to figure it out.

But first, he had to get his shit together. No serious conversation should begin with someone dressed only in a towel, hair still dripping wet. He toweled off, fixing his hair, and threw on the most festive outfit he had, including his Santa hat and the final sweater he'd brought with him, featuring an entire Santa's Workshop scene, complete with glittery snow, jingle bells, and brightly dressed elves making toys and caring for reindeer. It was ridiculous, impossibly detailed, and the single best example of tacky holiday wear he'd ever seen, so of course, he loved it. He imagined Jacob taking one look at it, rolling his eyes, and willing himself not to laugh. Owen smiled. He hoped it would raise Jacob's spirits.

He rushed to repack his bags. Somehow he couldn't make everything fit, despite the fact that it all came out of them to begin with. He tried several different configurations, including stuffing socks and underwear into jeans' pockets, and even rolling everything into tight balls. Finally, he managed to make space for everything. As he was packing the last few pieces of clothing away, he picked up the sweater that Jacob had worn all day yesterday. He pushed the button in the sleeve and smiled as he thought of Jacob whistling along to the familiar tune. Suddenly, an idea popped into his head. He set the sweater on the bed and headed out toward the lobby.

He had to find something to wrap a present in. Luckily, Jacob was apparently in the office, so he didn't have to worry about spoiling the surprise, but he needed to ask someone for help.

"Hey, Mandy!" Owen called to the housekeeper as she was making a beeline for the door. "Can you help me for a minute?"

"Oh, sorry. The roads are clear and Elk Terrace is closing for Christmas. I was just leaving. Enjoy your-"

"It will only take a second, I promise," Owen cut her off. "Please? It's for Jake."

Mandy huffed, but Jacob had told him that she was enthusiastic about them getting together, so when she didn't immediately walk out, he knew he had her.

"Fine, whatever. I'm listening," she said in the most impatient voice Owen had heard from her yet.

"Do you guys have any gift wrap and tape lying around? I'm trying to make something special to give to Jake."

"Well, this is a hotel, and despite what the past few days may lead you to believe, no one actually lives here, so no, we don't keep wrapping paper in the supply closet. Tape I can get you." She led him over to the desk and tossed a roll of scotch tape in his general direction.

"Thanks, Mandy," Owen said, a little defeated.

"Listen, I don't know what happened, but something has him even mopier than usual. You should talk to him."

"Yeah, I will. Thanks."

"Merry Christmas, Owen. And good luck."

"Merry Christmas."

With that, Mandy practically ran out the door before any of the other guests streaming into the lobby to check out could stop her.

Owen felt a little lost. He had this great idea, and now it seemed like he wouldn't get a chance to make it happen. He looked around the lobby, searching for some inspiration. Almost out of nowhere, he spotted a magazine rack by the sitting area near the fireplace and a light bulb went off in his head. *They won't mind if I tear up a few of those if it means salvaging Jake's Christmas.* He collected two of the least Jacob-like magazines, the most recent *People* and an old *Entertainment Weekly*, and hurried back to his room, breezing right past the various guests who called their goodbyes and holiday wishes after him. He was on a mission, and he couldn't let them distract him from it.

When he got back to his room, he quickly skimmed the magazines for the articles he knew would get under Jacob's skin the best. He found a massive profile of an old *Bachelor* contestant, a gaudy ad for the newest iPhone that made even him grimace, and something about Gwyneth Paltrow's next bougie wellness scheme. He hoped Jacob would find them all hilariously insipid. He hated wrapping clothing without a gift box to put it in, because you could never make it look pretty. Still, he tried everything he could to force the lumpy mess into something vaguely present-shaped, and set out to find Jacob.

He waited by the fire for the flurry of people clamoring to check out and get on the road. Jacob looked overwhelmed and more annoyed than usual as the guests argued over minibar charges and missing towels. Owen wanted to rush up there and help, but he didn't know the first thing about the process, and he figured the most helpful thing he could do was just be patient and stay out of the way, so he put his feet up and passed the time writing a glowing Yelp review for Elk Terrace Lodge.

Finally, the last guests, the McIntyres, managed to pry their children's heads out of their phones and headed out to the parking lot, waving goodbye and wishing happy holidays. He walked to the desk, gift in hand.

"All set to check out?" Jacob said in a tired sigh, rubbing his eyes.

Owen was taken aback by the blasé tone in his voice. Did the fact that their time together was over mean nothing to him?

"Almost," Owen began cautiously. "I had something I wanted to give you before I leave."

Jacob looked up at him then, his eyes quizzical but reserved.

"Really?" He sounded disbelieving. "Uh, okay. Do you keep spare gifts in your bags in case you meet a random stranger on the road on Christmas?"

"Something like that," Owen answered, choosing to ignore the barb of accusation in Jacob's question. "Here. Open it and see."

Jacob took the gift and just as he hoped, Owen saw him roll his eyes at the choice of gift wrap. He took particular care to start the unwrapping by punching a hole in the Bachelor's face with his thumb. Owen couldn't hold back a sharp, breathy chuckle at his completely predictable behavior. Jacob tore away the paper and held up the Rudolph sweater. Owen reached to press the button, and the tinny music filled the silence that thickened around them. Jacob smiled drearily and let the sweater drop onto the desk as the last few notes rang out in the stillness.

"Owen, I can't accept this," Jacob said just above a whisper.

"Why not?"

"Because it's yours," Jacob said. "Because I didn't get you anything," he tried when his first attempt wasn't getting anywhere. Owen still wasn't letting him off the hook. "Because I don't-"

"Because you don't what?"

"Nevermind, I just can't."

"No. I can't accept *that*. You don't what, Jake?"

Jacob growled in frustration, turning his back on Owen for a moment.

"Because I don't want to be stuck with a souvenir constantly reminding me I'm never gonna see you again."

Owen took a step back and tried to process what he just said.

"Jake, I didn't mean-" He trailed off. He really didn't know what to say to that, but he didn't get a chance to think about it.

"Look, I had a lot of fun this week. More than I usually

do out here, for sure. But it wasn't real life. The roads are open now, you're free to go back to your normal life, while I stay here and live mine, where I make a point of not falling in love with guests who happen to stay longer than two nights. We live completely different lives, Owen. I've never even been to Denver, and you hate being out here in the sticks. Ergo, we can't just throw caution to the wind and be together, obstacles and consequences be damned, so I'd rather not be reminded of that, so thanks, but no."

Owen tried to take in everything Jacob was saying. If he were being honest, he had to fight to keep listening after the whole "falling in love with guests" part; his mind tried to run away with thoughts of New Year's and Valentine's Days spent with each other, going on cheesy dates that one of them would plan just because they knew the other would hate it, of moving in together, maybe adopting a pet, waking up every morning in each other's arms...

Owen snapped back to reality. Jacob had somehow managed to convince himself that they would never see each other again, but that idea never occurred to Owen. He didn't want to drive away and consign this week to some vague, pleasant memory of a time he hooked up with a hotel manager on Christmas Eve. This meant something to Owen. *Jacob* meant something to Owen, and he knew that he meant something to Jacob too. He had to find a way to communicate that.

"Come to my parents' for dinner with me," he blurted out without really thinking.

"What?" Jacob looked thrown off by the non sequitur, so Owen tried to clarify.

"I don't want this to be a one-time thing." He tried to convey his earnestness and desperation in his voice. "I know this whole weekend was a weird fluke, and that we both have to get back to real life, and those lives are about as different as they get, but I don't care about any of that. Somehow we managed to build something between us, and I think it has the potential to be really special, so I'm not just gonna pull out of here and pretend to be all joyous and festive with my family without you there."

"Owen, we can't just-"

"I know it's a bit early to meet the parents." Owen refused to let him finish that sentence. "But no one should be alone on Christmas, and I'm not ready for this unreal, serendipitous, completely fucking magical week to be over yet. So pack your shit, and let's go. My parents do dinner at four, and we've still got a bit of a drive."

Jacob bounded around the desk and pulled Owen into a kiss so passionate and intense, he knew that Jacob was feeling exactly the same about him. They kissed for a long minute, embracing so tightly it might have been uncomfortable were they not so desperate to be as close to each other as possible. Owen was completely out of breath when Jacob suddenly pulled away with a guilty expression.

"But...I can't go with you. I have to go check on Ethel. I need to make sure she's okay, and that she has everything she needs."

"Fuck it. Let's bring her along," Owen said, in full-on problem-solving mode. "So long as she doesn't mind a couple of rowdy kids, a hyperactive beagle, and cranberry sauce tart enough to keep you puckering all night."

"Really?" Jacob asked, astounded. "Your parents would be okay with you rolling in with two complete strangers in tow?"

"Oh, Mom makes enough food to fatten up all of Eagle County. Besides, if we get all of the meet-the-parents awkwardness out of the way at once, we won't have to cringe our way through some uncomfortable third degree over Easter dinner."

Jacob gave Owen a bright-eyed smile at his understanding that he viewed Ethel as a kind of adoptive mother. He leaned in to kiss Owen again.

"I think I might really like you, Owen," Jacob said tenderly. "You're not bad for a stuck-up city boy who's head over heels for vapid holiday commercialism."

"I think I might really like you, too," Owen said, planting a quick kiss on Jacob's lips. "Even though you're a bitter, grumpy Hermit of the Hills who can't even hang a Christmas tree star on straight." Owen nodded in the direction of the tree and its indeed crooked star. Jacob sneered at him but caught him up in a kiss all the same.

"Seriously, we gotta go," Owen barked, his tone all business now. "If we hurry, we can still make the kids digging into their stockings. Get your shit and let's hit the road."

Jacob hurried to the office, and came back holding a backpack and a set of keys, pulling his coat on as he walked. Owen grabbed his hand, lacing their fingers together, and pulled him toward the door. Jacob flipped the light switch on their way out, stopped to lock the door, and soon enough they were pulling out of the parking lot, speeding off to salvage what was left of Christmas together.

EPILOGUE

Jacob heard four furious knocks on the bedroom door. Owen was getting antsy, like he usually did whenever Ethel came over for dinner and immediately pushed him out of the kitchen so she could bake something incredible.

"Mom just called," Owen shouted through the door. He sounded more stressed than Jacob had ever heard. "They'll be here in five minutes."

"I'll be done in a second," Jacob shouted back. "Why don't you go obsessively rearrange the Christmas village figurines for the ninetieth time?"

"Ho, ho, ho," Owen said, dripping with sarcasm.

Jacob actually thought it was cute that Owen couldn't decide if the little ceramic bakery looked better next to the snow-covered church or the North Pole Express train station. He had more than come around Owen's excessive holiday cheer in the year since they were trapped in the hotel, which Owen had turned into a regular winter wonderland without his consent. Ok, without his *enthusiastic* consent. Like he could say no to the man who acted like an overgrown workshop elf from Halloween to New Year's. Shit, he was pretty much like that for every holiday, not just Christmas. St. Patrick's Day was nothing but a sea of green, glittery shamrocks, buckets full of fake gold nuggets under rainbows, and enough Guiness and Bailey's to drown half of Denver. He wouldn't even speak about Valentine's Day, which involved so much chocolate and red wine that he couldn't even remember if they'd actually stayed in bed all day, or if he'd just blacked out for everything else.

But this was their first Christmas together. They made the decision to move in together on Halloween, and they finally found a decent apartment in a small outer suburb about halfway between the hotel and Owen's job in Denver. If Owen had to swear to it in court, he could admit that he enjoyed not paying rent for his downtown loft, and Jacob was finally making some headway in convincing him to appreciate what he and Ethel called "small-town charm." For some reason, they decided to invite his entire family, along with Ethel and Mandy, for a Christmas dinner housewarming combination party. Normally Jacob was the one to stress about having that many people in his house, but today Owen was one disaster away from a full-on panic attack. He had to physically move the punch bowl of Grandma Campbell's atomic eggnog onto the balcony before Owen accidentally got completely wasted.

"They are pulling into the lot as we speak!" Owen sounded desperate now.

"I'm putting the finishing touches on right now," Jacob insisted. He felt bad for locking Owen out of their bedroom, but it was the only way to stop this exact behavior from ruining the surprise. "Give me thirty seconds!"

"You have fifteen!"

Jacob rolled his eyes as he tied the ribbon on his carefully wrapped gift into a big, festive bow. He'd been so nervous about what to get Owen for Christmas. They agreed not to spend too much because they had to drop a bunch of money on the deposit for the apartment and furnishing the place. Jacob had lived in a one-room apartment above someone's garage a few minutes from Elk Terrace, so he didn't really have anything to contribute to a joint household. He expected Owen to have his fancy downtown loft decked out like an HGTV show, so he was shocked when they went back to Owen's place for the first time and he only saw a handful of mismatched pieces that looked like they'd followed Owen right from a secondhand shop, through years of student housing abuse, and up to his bougie highrise where they stood out like a sore thumb.

So he tried to think small for a gift this year, but what do you get for a man that waits for Christmas like a ghost waits for Halloween? Everything he came up with was either too expensive or too tacky. He struck gold when he was able to coax Owen's sister, Zoe, to tell him that he was planning on giving Jacob 'something that reminded him of when they met.' That gave Jacob an idea. He scoured every shop and website he could find from Halloween to Thanksgiving searching for the gaudiest, most festive, most Owen-like Christmas sweater he could find, but all of the best patterns only came in children's sizes. Finally he stumbled on an Etsy store that offered custom Christmas sweaters, "guaranteed to arrive by the twenty-fifth or your money back." He ordered the most obnoxious pattern he could think of and waited anxiously for it to arrive. Jacob heard the door buzzer sound, and he hurried to unlock and open the door right as Owen started a new round of frantic knocking. Jacob had to take a step back to avoid getting hit as Owen's knuckles sailed right through the space where the door was half a second ago.

"Jesus, I'm ready!" said Jacob, hiding the present behind his back with a mischievous smile.

Owen let loose an exasperated sigh and went to open the front door for his family. Jacob rushed to sneak the present under the tree while Owen was distracted, earning a judgemental smirk from Mandy who was lounging on the sofa apparently very involved in whatever was happening on her phone. He shot her back a lighthearted, if withering, look as was their typical exchange whenever he did something that Mandy considered 'nauseatingly romantic.' He knew that she completely supported his relationship with Owen. Some days when they worked together, she would make comments like how she was glad Owen was around to keep him busy so he wasn't haunting the halls of the hotel like some low-rent Ghost of Christmas Future. He was *almost* certain that meant she was happy for him.

He could hear Owen's nephews' ruckus down the hall, and Zoe's desperate attempts to silence them, so per their agreement, he retrieved the eggnog from outside, practically begged Ethel to stop frosting cookies and go put her feet up, and then slid his hand into Owen's, ready to greet his family in the doorway.

～

Dinner was fantastic, thanks to the combined, if somewhat disjointed, efforts of Owen and Ethel. Somehow they'd managed to fit an entire turkey and ham, along with some kind of vegetarian roast thing for Mandy, six different sides, including a massive dish of dressing, cooked outside the bird at Mandy's request, three pies, a roll cake, and about four dozen cookies, which Ethel seemed to have whipped up, baked, and decorated all in under an hour. Jacob wondered, not for the first time, if Ethel was actually some kind of witch who used her powers exclusively to churn out the most incredible food you could imagine. Jacob didn't need to wonder if Owen was magical in some way. He managed to prove that every day they were together. The thought brought a warm smile to Jacob's face, and he caught Owen's eye across the table. Owen smiled back, winking before returning to his mother and Ethel debate the various degrees of bad weather Colorado had seen in the past thirty years, and whether last year's whiteout even broke into the top ten.

Mandy found some unexpected common ground with Owen's father talking about how 'the dumbasses in this administration won't be happy until they ruin the lives of anyone who isn't a millionaire.' Jacob initially tried to steer their conversation away from politics, out of fear that Mandy would start some fight about welfare policy or something, but he was pleasantly surprised when they got along like a house on fire, as Ethel would say.

All in all, the evening was perfect, and around the time the fourth bottle of wine was opened, Jacob finally let himself exhale. He almost couldn't believe how different this Christmas was from any of the years he'd spent with his parents. Everyone was happy, laughing, and glad to be around each other. Ethel even started belting out carols along with the Yule Log track after she'd had a glass and a half of what she called the devil's own eggnog, and declaring her lifelong respect and warmest regards to the memory of Grandma Campbell.

Finally, when Owen couldn't force anyone to eat another crumb of pie, or drink even a tablespoon more wine, Jacob announced it was time to open presents. Everyone got up from the table and managed to find places to sit in the living room. He assigned Mandy the task of passing out the gifts, as the furniture was distributed based on seniority, which left her on the floor anyway. He and Owen had taken care to get everyone something, not just the kids, for whom Owen had about fifteen boxes apiece. Jacob brought an empty wastebasket in for all the wrapping paper, then he sat down half on Owen's lap and handed him the gift he'd been working on.

It was a thin box wrapped in pages of outdoors magazines, sporting goods catalogs, and even a printed-out blog post about doomsday prepping, which he knew Owen hated more than just about anything else. It was his payback for the tabloid-wrapped gift he'd received last year. The tag read "To Rudolph, Love, your Abominable Snowman." Owen turned bright red at the chorus of awes that erupted around the room. He gave Jacob a little kiss on the cheek before tearing open the package. Inside was a Christmas sweater in the most garish Christmas red he could find, and on it was a disgruntled-looking yeti, scowling as an elf tried to place a Santa hat on his head.

"So everyone can see what the holidays are like at our house," Jacob said.

Owen lifted his chin into a real kiss, earning a pronounced 'EEEWW!' from his nephews, and Jacob could swear he heard Mandy join in. Jacob proudly proclaimed himself the winner of this year's gift giving, even though he did love the bottle of the same brand of peppermint schnapps they'd drank the night they shared their first kiss.

The evening went more perfectly than either of them had hoped. Everyone was full, happy, and thankful for the time they shared together. After the last of the dishes were loaded into the dishwasher, and the last goodbyes said, followed by a heated spat between Owen and Zoe about whether she would bring home the rest of the cookies for the boys to eat, which Owen finally won by attrition, then another round of goodbyes, well wishes, and thanks, they were finally alone again. Jacob pulled Owen into a long, loving, incredibly exhausted kiss.

"Merry Christmas, babe," Owen said, breaking the kiss, but then pressing another soft kiss into Jacob's forehead.

"Merry Christmas, Owen."

AFTERWORD

If you enjoyed this book, please consider leaving a review on Amazon! It helps readers discover the book, and is a great way to show your support!

You can also subscribe to C.M. Valencourt's newsletter! You'll get the latest updates about upcoming releases and sales, plus bonus content and other goodies! When you subscribe, you'll also receive a sweet, free m/m short story. To subscribe, visit cmvalencourt.com/newsletter.

Keep reading for an excerpt of C.M. Valencourt's debut novel *From the Ashes*!

FROM THE ASHES

EXCERPT

CHAPTER 1

*D*erek knew if he had just a little bit more time, he could make the scene work.

"Let's do one more take," he called, and the actress hastily let go of her scene partner, taking a sidestep to the left.

The actors in the short film—*his* short film—had been a nightmare all day. They had zero chemistry but they were the only theatre majors who'd come out to the casting call. They probably needed the acting experience for one of *their* classes. The film was due next week, which barely gave the editors and color correctors and sound guys enough time to do their thing.

"It's almost dark," Alison, his assistant director, said from behind the monitors. "The lighting's gonna be shit."

It's either the lighting or the acting, Derek thought. They hadn't gotten a believable take of the final romantic scene, where Kenny quits his job and offers to move across the country with Abigail. Derek needed to show that he could work with even the most difficult actors if he wanted to pass the class and have something good to put in his directing portfolio. He wouldn't turn in something mediocre just because it was easier. Even though he'd already put in some applications for some top-tier fellowships, his best chance of moving to LA with something lined up was to make sure this film and his senior project were solid.

Derek loved all sorts of film, and his undergrad degree had definitely taught him how to direct the sort of films that would be shown at festivals—artsy pieces about Paris or divorce, or getting divorced *in Paris*. He liked making those films, but Derek was the most drawn to horror movies.

He'd seen his first real horror film with his friends Justin and Hunter when they were twelve. Justin, like apparently every other guy in the United States in 2009, was in love with Megan Fox, so he'd convinced his friends to buy a ticket to *Ice Age: Dawn of the Dinosaurs* but then sneak into *Jennifer's Body* instead. All three of them had been surprised when the movie hadn't been the soft porn flick they expected, but was actually funny and bloody and so over the top that Hunter actually dug his nails into Derek's arm when the black sludge started gushing out of her mouth.

From there, they'd watched every horror flick they could get their hands on, from *Rosemary's Baby* and *The Shining* on DVD to the midnight releases of *Insidious* and *Paranormal Activity 3*. Horror movies turned into their thing. But Derek did more than just watch them; he studied each film, analyzing what made it great and wondering how he could make it better. Sometimes he even took notes, and he didn't care that his friends teased him.

Derek loved making movies, and it drove him crazy that he wasn't particularly good at it yet. His films weren't ready to go to festivals or win awards or even to go straight to DVD. He knew he would get better—that was the point of the prestigious art school that his parents were shelling out a staggering amount of money for—but he was excited for the point in his career when he could direct a film that consisted of more than some crappy aspiring actors and a rented light kit. And he hoped, maybe after his fellowship, he could finally make a movie with some fake blood.

"I don't think we have it yet," Derek said, trying not to let annoyance creep into his voice while also remaining firm. He wanted his directing style to be encouraging; he wanted to push the actors and make them better, but also be able to go out to coffee with them after a long day of filming. He certainly didn't want to be one of those directors who screamed at his actors on-set and showed up on *Entertainment Tonight* throwing a bagel at a costume designer.

"We had a good last take," the girl playing Abigail whined.

"Let's just do one more to be safe," Derek said. He wasn't going to budge on this.

She rolled her eyes. "Fine, but I'm not spending my entire Saturday night making out with this guy in a parking lot." She turned to her fellow actor. "No offense."

"Hey, getting your drool all over my face isn't my first choice for a Saturday night, either," the guy playing Kenny retorted. "And you promised there would be pizza!" he called to Derek.

"There *will* be pizza," Derek said as they reset and the makeup girl did last looks, applying yet another coat of lipstick to Abigail's lips. He would order it once everything was over, as everyone's reward for actually getting a good take.

"Action!" Derek called, putting on his earpiece.

Derek watched as Abigail walked across the parking lot, suitcase in hand. She was sure Kenny wouldn't follow her, so she had given up hope, all business now. Her plane left soon, and she was determined to leave on it, not caring that she was leaving the love of her life behind.

But suddenly, Kenny was behind her, grabbing her wrist. He had his own suitcase. Both of them were actually empty, of course, but Derek imagined that Kenny had packed only whatever his hands came to first in his bedroom, and he had an unmanageable assortment of clothes; they'd have to go to a clothing store the second that they landed, but he didn't care. He had to get to the airport.

The girl playing Abigail managed to look genuinely surprised to see Kenny in this take, her mouth forming an O shape, and when he pulled her in for a kiss, she was enthusiastic this time, thank god; he thought he even saw a bit of her tongue go into Kenny's mouth.

Derek hadn't written the script, but he liked the longing in it, Abigail's willingness to forgive Kenny's past mistakes, the way that Kenny was brave enough to try to stop her from getting away. He hoped they captured all of that tonight, because the lighting really was going to be shit if they did another take.

"Alright, we can wrap," he said. "Thank you so much for putting up with all of the takes, and for being such a kickass crew. I'll order pizza for anyone who wants to stick around."

The actors playing Kenny and Abigail high-fived, and the tech workers started coiling cables and taking down lights.

Derek got out his phone. He was about to call the pizza place when he noticed that he had three missed calls, all from his mother.

Derek's mom almost never called him. Although he'd moved across the country for college, from small-town Ohio to Boston, they weren't exactly the thrice-weekly-Skype-call kind of family. Derek stayed out of trouble and got good grades, and in exchange, his parents wrote big checks for everything from his tuition to all the latest Blu-Rays he needed for "research" to impromptu pizza for his film crew.

He knew he should just call for the pizza before his actors got openly hostile, but his imagination was getting the best of him now. He couldn't remember the last time his mom had called him instead of just sending a text message.

He dialed her number and waited, his heart beating loud in his ears. Finally, she picked up.

"Mom, are you okay?" Derek asked, a small tremor in his intonation.

There was a pause that lasted long enough that Derek was about to ask again to make sure someone was there. "I'm fine," his mother answered, her tone serious. "But Derek, something's happened. Have you been online?"

Derek hadn't had a lot of time to browse Facebook lately, the film consuming most of the time he wasn't spending in a classroom. If he wasn't on the set, he was thinking about the movie. He'd even made a mood board about Kenny's emotional journey last week.

"No, I haven't. I've been on set. What's the-"

"Honey, you might want to go somewhere quiet for a minute. It's about Justin. Justin Sweeney."

Of course he knew which Justin she meant. Justin, who he'd played middle school baseball with until they'd both quit after one month, because they preferred staying inside and watching movies, and they were both scared of the fly balls anyways. Justin, who used to convince him and Hunter to sneak out of their parents' houses at night, just so they could drive around and use the swings at the local playground. Justin, who won both Most Likely to Succeed and Class Clown in the yearbook.

For a moment, he wondered why his mother had bothered saying his last name.

But then he remembered how old those memories were, remembered that he and Justin hadn't talked—*really* talked—in years.

"Okaaay.... What's up with Justin?"

It must just be some sort of gossip, he thought. Maybe Justin was getting married, or had knocked someone up. There wasn't much else to do in Akron, Ohio.

"Derek...Justin passed away last night."

Derek almost dropped his phone. *What?*

"That can't be right. Justin *Sweeney*? You must have him confused with someone else." She had to mean some other Justin, maybe someone he'd gone to preschool with or one of his father's friends.

"No, honey. The Justin from high school. He had cancer."

Derek took a breath, trying to make sense of this. "I didn't even know he was sick."

"I didn't, either. I think he and his mother wanted to keep it quiet. Maybe they thought he would get better." He could hear his mother's high heels clicking in the background as she paced around the hardwood floor of the kitchen. He was silent. "His mother called me and was insistent you come back for the funeral; she said Justin wanted you there. He wanted you to have something, too. Your father and I will fly you out, of course, but you'll need to head to the airport early tomorrow morning."

He didn't even think about the film, that he should be there in the editing room, that he wanted to be able to micromanage every moment of the film's life. All that he could think about was that Justin was dead, and he hadn't even told Derek he was sick. Was it because he didn't want to trouble Derek at his fancy East Coast school? Justin had always called it "fancy," like he and his roommates were drinking vintage bordeaux out of goblets in the dining hall.

Or had Justin not even thought that Derek would care that he was dying?

Derek cared. He cared a lot.

But none of this made sense. None of it seemed real. He looked over at his cast and crew, half expecting them to be different, to somehow know what was happening. But they were still standing around, making small talk and waiting for the pizza. Everything was the same. He felt his stomach flip over.

"Okay. I'll come. Obviously I'll come. Can you text me the flight info? I- I have to go."

His mother agreed, and he hung up the phone, his stomach roiling.

"Hey, did you order the pizza yet, Mr. Director?" Alison asked, suddenly behind him at the bank of monitors. "The crew wants two with extra bacon."

He couldn't really hear her.

She couldn't have meant *Justin*. There must have been a mistake. *Is this what being in shock feels like?*

He turned to Alison, his thoughts jumbled: the fact that he'd already played the last video game with his friend, and he couldn't even remember what it was; the cancer that had started somewhere small inside Justin and then eaten all the way through him; and the extra bacon, the grease, the smell.

Derek turned around, looked at Alison, and threw up all over her Doc Martens.

CHAPTER 2

It took three tries for Hunter to tie the black bowtie in the department store dressing room, his hands were shaking so badly.

He didn't have a suit to wear to Justin's service. Why would he have one? He was too young for friends' weddings, and much too young for friends' funerals.

He'd tried on a few solemn grey and black suits, but all he could think about when he put them on was how they would look buried in the back of his closet, always the suit that he'd gone to his high school best friend's memorial service in. Solemn, useless, a permanent reminder.

Hunter had spent most of the last couple of days wallowing, alternating between being pissed at Justin and being pissed off at himself for being pissed at Justin. Who was he to try to tell Justin how he should have had cancer? But he couldn't help but wonder what would have happened if Justin had told him, had let him in. He would have been able to see him one last time, at least, but he hoped that it could have been more, that they could have put all of the stupidity behind them, really been friends again.

Justin's memorial page online was well-populated with notes. In high school, Justin had been the specific type of popular where everyone would wish him a happy birthday on Facebook, but the only people he really hung out with were Hunter and Derek. By the number of notes, he seemed to have kept this up in college, too. He'd had a girlfriend who wrote a truly heartbreaking letter on his page so long that the website made her post it in three parts. Hunter noticed a lot of posts from people who lived in Akron who definitely hadn't known Justin very well but were talking about how upset they were. He had typed up a few comments to their posts, asking if they knew even one thing about who Justin had been, but he never sent them.

He hadn't been able to make himself write his own note on the site. What would he even write? *Sorry we all grew apart because of my stupid mistake? Sorry I couldn't keep my feelings to myself? Sorry it was too hard for me to hang out with you, even though you probably didn't even know why we stopped being friends?*

Hunter had been best friends with Justin for years, inseparable from him and Derek since they were twelve. Justin was one of the most extroverted people Hunter had ever met, even sometimes to a fault. The first week of middle school, the three of them had ended up at the same lunch table, unsure of their place in the new social order. Hunter hadn't really been close with any of the kids in his elementary —he suspected they could sense the homosexuality before he did and steered clear accordingly—so he ended up at the reject's table. Derek was there because he'd come from a Catholic school, and Justin's mom had moved to a new school district after the divorce. Justin had been the first one to make conversation, talking about the part he was on in

Dragon Age, and before any of them knew it, they were friends.

Hunter stepped out of the dressing room, doing a melancholic flourish with his hands for Julia.

"What do you think?" he asked.

"It doesn't exactly scream funeral," Julia said, biting her lip.

To be fair, it didn't. It was a bit tacky, black with darker black rose blooms printed all over it, the bowtie really driving the whole thing home.

"Justin didn't even have the decency to tell me he was fucking dying, Jules," he said, not quiet enough for the space or the setting, his hands balled into fists. "I should at least be able to wear something that I don't hate to his funeral."

"Woah," Julia said, putting her hands up in a makeshift barrier between her and her brother.

In truth, he was putting up a fight because this suit made him feel safe, even though he knew it would make several of Justin's older relatives gossip. Let them. He wanted to be who he really was when he saw Justin for the last time, faggy statement print and all.

Hunter softened, as much as he could. "I'm sorry. I just- this is going to be a whole production."

Julia put a hand on her brother's back. "What do you mean?"

He sighed. "Well, I'm going to cry like a vegan in a meatpacking plant, first of all. It's not going to be pretty." He paused. "Secondly, there are going to be people there that I'd...rather not see."

"You're nervous about seeing Derek?" Julia asked. In a weak (and very drunk) moment, he'd told Julia about everything that had gone down with Derek. *Stupid, stupid.*

Hunter went back into the changing room and began taking off the bowtie.

Hunter hadn't seen Derek since he'd fled all the way to Boston to escape him. He'd started letters, Facebook messages, even considered dropping by his house on holiday break, but in the end, he'd chickened out. And now it had been so long that the animosity between them had really had some time to develop a smell.

Unlike Derek, Hunter had gone to college in Cleveland, less than an hour away from Akron. He didn't have the easy excuses not to see Justin that Derek had. But after Derek and Hunter's falling out, Justin made it his mission to fix the problem between them, even though he never knew the whole story, never knew the feeling Hunter got in his chest every time Justin mentioned Derek to him. Justin had even maintained a group Facebook message between all three of them for a while that only he ever posted in, funny memes and YouTube videos. Eventually, though, he seemed to get the picture, and all three of them had stopped talking, even though they had been such a huge part of each other's lives, had promised each other really sentimental things that they'd deny if anyone called them on it, like groomsmen and apartments on the West Coast and stupid things like "bros for life."

He could have seen Justin at any time, called him up and been at their favorite coffee house in an hour. He just hadn't, because of everything with Derek.

"I'm not nervous," he called out to Julia. "I just don't wanna see his stupid fucking face."

"Very mature," Julia said from the other side of the door.

"I mean it. I'm not planning to say one word to the guy."

This day was about Justin. Sure, he would see Derek

there, assuming he even cared enough to show up. But it had been too long. There was nothing to say.

"You could probably help each other, you know. You were all so close. He's probably feeling the same grief you are."

And the same guilt, Hunter thought, peeling off the tightly-fitted suit pants.

"I don't need his help."

He took care to hang the suit properly on the hanger, even though the girl at the register would probably take it off and throw it in a shopping bag anyway.

This day is about Justin, he reminded himself. *Not your stupid high school drama.*

ABOUT THE AUTHOR

C.M. Valencourt is a new m/m romance author. They started devouring queer fiction when they still had to smuggle it into their parents' Catholic household, and dreamed of writing books about queer people finding love ever since. They like figure skating, ghost hunting shows, and Carly Rae Jepsen. You can find out more about their books and learn about upcoming releases at cmvalencourt.com

ALSO BY C.M. VALENCOURT

From the Ashes

Printed in Great Britain
by Amazon